I0622259

…If low self-esteem did not exist, this world would be without bad women…

August, 2013

ImmigranT:OrgonE

Bojana Tokic

INTRODUCTION

I am here to tell the life story of a woman with the biggest heart that ever existed in the United States. She is a killer, prostitute, liar, thief, and manipulator. Yet, she is a better woman than any other woman in this country.

I met her the day she was born, but I never wanted to approach her until her biggest fear came true and the only way for her to survive was by accepting me. She is strong mentally and physically; both necessary for fulfilling her destiny. The beginning of her life was not smooth, but the end was even rougher than God expected it to be.

It is not easy to explain her actions, because her priorities do not correspond to the significances of the majority. Every move was led by love or unexplainable fear, and many terrors lived in her heart without her acknowledgment. Eventually, most of them became reality.

BOOK 1

CHAPTER 1

Snow blizzards are so beautiful under the moon's light. Snowflakes are running in a circle and it looks like they want to move and stay still at the same time. They are lovely and playful. You are happy to see them, because you picture snowmen, sledding, snow fights, snow angels...Now stop and think this way: transportation delays, electricity outages, falls, school cancellations, taking off from work...Don't ever think that something beautiful can't hurt you.

The Doll House, a four year old place, is located in Oneonta, New York. It is not an easy place to find, but if you get there once, you will be able to find it a second time without a struggle. The outside of the house is pink with hints of purple around the windows.

On the first floor is a bar. Beautiful girls are serving drinks while providing a relaxing atmosphere through dance and songs. The walls are black and the entire bar is white with red candles on it. It is a little dark inside, but bright enough to enjoy the shapes of the gorgeous ladies. In front of the bar are two rows containing three tables, each with big red candles. It is just a regular small bar with very sexy girls.

To get to the second and third floors, you have to use the outside steps which are located on the opposite side of the bar entry. On the second floor is a huge bedroom with a king size bed in the middle of the room. An enormous Jacuzzi is a few feet away from the foot of the bed. The bedroom door is facing the right side of the bed. On the

1

wall, across from the door, is a large window that faces the parking lot. A small oval coffee table, surrounded with four chairs, is positioned a few feet away from the door. A fridge, with a sink next to it, is on the right side of the door. The small bathroom is on the left. Across from the bed is a long closet. The owner lives on this floor and this space is used as a bedroom, as well as the office. The third floor is just an empty space with separate small storage rooms.

Powerful men from New York City, Bridge Hampton, Westchester and Albany visit at least twice a month. It depends how great their lust is. This place is well-known in rich circles, but it is kept as a secret. It is known for its girls. They dance in elegant clothing while accompanied by tunes of Mozart, Beethoven, Bach and Sinatra. The only drink available is an expensive wine. You will not find this kind of place anywhere else in the world.

The third floor is also used for other kind of dancers to perform. Every night, there are a few out of seven great-looking men performing. If they get paid generously, they might go inside a small storage room with a customer to pleasure him as long as his heart desires. The music is loud enough to keep the noise unnoticeable and the storage room is big enough for one full size mattress to keep the couple comfortable.

There are two rules in The Doll House: you have to wear a mask on your face for your privacy and have a lot of money to show gratitude.

The snow didn't stop the politician from NYC, in the mask from Phantom of the Opera, to show up early for his very own session with his favorite doll, DaxoN. DaxoN is over six feet tall, a muscular, pale boy, with dirty blonde hair. His blue eyes can hypnotize you immediately. This relationship has been going on almost four years. They upgraded their love to the second floor. The owner was nice enough to let them use it for their "love explosion". In return, the politician kindly leaves the fat envelope on the desk for the owner. Usually, there is between ten and twenty thousand dollars inside.

The room is almost completely dark. That way, the politician can take off the mask, and still not be recognized. You are able to see the shadows and feel the movements. They were kissing, touching each other's bodies and getting lost in lust. DaxoN stretched his arm to turn on the lamp, but the politician's reflexes were fast enough to grab his hand before the light destroyed his entire life. The politician held DaxoN's hand very firmly for a few seconds and then placed it between his legs, so DaxoN could get back to pleasuring him.

The camera above the entrance door was able to manipulate the dark and capture the face of the well-known politician. The owner kept the tapes as her own insurance, in case she ever needed blackmailing material.

The moon was high in the sky. The snow was crystal clear and shades of many trees formed patterns on the white ground. How beautiful this world is! And she lives an ugly life in it... She is the owner of The Doll House.

***

At midnight, the politician left Oneonta. DaxoN was sitting in the Jacuzzi when the owner walked in; a woman in her early thirties. She has a modest appearance. She is fake blonde, tall, skinny and owns a strong facial expression. She is wearing black leggings and an oversized grey sweatshirt. Her long blonde hair is all over the place.

You could say she is pretty and sexy, very sexy. Her accent is strong and her voice is loud.

- What are you still doing here? If you do not have any more clients, go to sleep in the car or maybe in the storage room until you excrete out the alcohol. Just leave from here, please. I am tired.

DAXON - I wanted to see his face and he got upset.

- You are so stupid, DaxoN. Come tomorrow morning to pick up your money and that is the only thing that should be seen; money has all kinds of faces.

DAXON - I've been sleeping with him for almost four years now and I've never seen him. He's a mystery to me, but not to my heart.

- DaxoN, that man comes here to have gay sex with you and you come here to earn big money. His privacy is protected and he can go out there and be whoever he wants to be and you can do the same. Remember, you cannot have feelings if you want to become rich and successful. Please, get out of here. I have to clean this, so I can go to sleep.

While she was changing the sheets on the bed, DaxoN didn't stop opening himself up to her, while still sitting in the Jacuzzi.

DAXON - His skin is so smooth. When he kisses me, my body shivers. My mind is filled with his voice and I can't wait to hold his face in my hands. I looked in his eyes and even though I wasn't able to see them in the dark, I was able to imagine our bright future.

- Enough with that crappy talk! DaxoN, you have five minutes to leave this room! Get yourself in control and

come back tomorrow night. Let me make something clear to you: You will never see his face and you will never have anything else with him besides what you have right now! In reality, he is your boss, not me. You get paid for the work that you do and there is no need to complicate this perfect affiliation. Many people never meet their boss and still they do their jobs. Now get up!

DAXON - Those are your words, not mine...or his. I will be out from here fast enough.

DaxoN left The Doll House with one wish in his heart: to see the face underneath the Phantom of the Opera mask.

That night, just for fun, two dolls went in the storage room with one client who at the end, gave extremely fat tips. Two hours after midnight, the business night ended. Only four clients arrived tonight and now they are gone. Not much happened this night.

She checked her inbox before being taken away by dreams. No emails from her sister. The bank statement ended up in a "junk" folder. Each time when she saw her bank card or the bank statement, she would be reminded of EdwarD. Everything was still in his name and there was no way to change it. To her surprise, there was an email from EdwarD. The time and place were the only things written, as it used to be years ago.

Her body stayed calm. Finally, after more than four years, he wants to see her. She won in this love war; he still needs her. Tomorrow she must get up early to fix herself. The point is not to show him how beautiful she is, but to prove to him how ugly his wife is compared to her.

5

As always, her emotions do not disturb her daily routine. She logged onto her Facebook account to post a few thoughts. Her Facebook was the only safe place where she was able to express her contemplations and get feedback, which she never read.

POST "RANDOM THOUGHTS" 58: *Who is the most important person in your life? Who do you live for? You have to take care of somebody to feel alive. You must begin from one individual and keep it as a base on which you will build strength to take care of others, with no limits for "how many", but yes for "how much".*

It is a remarkable ability in a human mind to mark events, things, people and even yourself as black or white; bad or good. In reality, there is no such thing. You must know some laws, so let's use a few of them as an example of my point.

Do not kill! You should never kill. If you follow this law, you are marked as a perfect follower of this particular rule. Are you marked as a good person also? What if I am a "good person", then I see somebody trying to kill my child and I intervene and accidentally murder that person? Am I a bad soul? If I didn't get involved and I just watched my child being killed, I would break another law: You are responsible for your child! (I don't care what you think about parenting, normal parents take care of their child and if you do not agree, you better change and start doing so.) You know all this and actually,

I will not go on and keep explaining the rules to you. You are smart and you can understand the point behind laws and rules. We need them as guidance and we have to know how to make a combination of them. If we drop a few of them, we are not black, nor if we respect them all; we are

6

not white. Remember, by following man's rules, we will break some of God's. The point is; we are gray and let's live with it!

Who are you? Who do you want to be? Why do you live? Let me make it clear to you; I am not here to feel sorry for you or to try to understand why you are who you are, and why you are not who you want to be. No one gives or sells confidence; you have to make it on your own! Good luck with that! Your dreams, sadness, aspirations and fears are not in your hands, legs, heart nor kidneys; it is in your head. Whatever you make out there in that head of yours, it will come out here, and you cannot stop it. Be careful what you think, very careful.

People of the United States of America! You are thankful every single day for living on this land, right? Yeah, right! If you do not like it, go away. You are already living somebody's dream by living here, so show some respect. This is the land of the opportunities, take what belongs to you and remember; there is plenty for all of us.

Do you want respect, power, admiration or maybe a position of a role model? You can have it. I can have it, too, as soon as we build something that all this will stand on. Knowledge! To get this, you must have an open mind. Oh yes, you do. Do you have it? Do you listen more or do you talk more? Make sure it is the first one. Do you spend more time answering questions or asking them? Make sure it is the second one. School will give you a lot of knowledge, but school alone is not enough. You have to read many books, watch television, get to know people and so much more to achieve true knowledge. To some people, being open-minded is second nature, and to others, it is a lesson to be learned.

Start from somewhere, right now. Take the closest book to you and read it. How many days will it take for you to finish it?

CHAPTER 2

Manhattan! Manhattan! The center of the world!
The most powerful place on this planet! Guess who is on a
boat with a view of this gorgeous city? Yes, she is. Not
alone, EdwarD is there, too. He took her for dinner on a
boat cruise and after, they will go to a nice hotel to have
some adult fun. At least that was his plan.

Manhattan was established in 1625. The name
Manhattan derives from the word "Manna-hata", as written
in the 1609 logbook of Robert Juet. The word "Manhattan"
has been translated as "island of many hills" from the
Lenape language.

When you come to this city, what are you going to
visit? You must see Times Square, Central Park, The
Empire State Building, The Statue of Liberty, The Brooklyn
Bridge, Grand Central, The Cathedral of Saint Patrick, The
World Trade Center, Rockefeller Center, The Stephen A.
Schwarzman Library and the stores on Fifth Ave.

Count how many races and nationalities you know.
How many different languages have you heard of? Well, all
your answers you can see and hear in Manhattan. When you
take a walk through this city, you are going to see every kind
of man and woman passing by in front of your eyes. In a
few cases, you will not even know if an individual is a man
or woman. Beautiful women in sizes from 0 to 52, ugly
women in sizes from 0 to 52, from very short to very tall,
from too nice to too bitchy and anything else that women can
be described by, is presented in Manhattan. The same goes
for men, too.

Look, there is a homeless person! Look, there is a billionaire! That man is famous and that woman over there is invisible. Don't step on her! Did you see the woman who just passed by you? She has two degrees and went all the way up on the academic ladder. Meanwhile, the man who is standing on your left never went to school. Oh Manhattan, how can you fit representatives of every person in human kind?

What are you hungry for? American, Chinese, French, Bosnian, Brazilian, Mexican, Russian, Italian, Caribbean, Turkish, Japanese, Arabic and every other cuisine that your stomach craves for can be found in Manhattan.

Shopping? Would you like to buy a shirt for one dollar or maybe a shirt that cost a hundred-thousand dollars? Brand names like Louis Vuitton, Prada, Coach, Gucci, Chanel, Fendi, Chloe, Dolce & Gabbana, Mulberry, Dior, and Calvin Klein all have a nice home in Manhattan; many of them more than one. Copies are very easy to find, too.

What is your religion? I can tell you which way to go and you will end up in front of your "prayer home". There, you are going to meet many people who share your beliefs. God is powerful! You don't believe in God? Don't worry, you will find plenty of people who are just like you.

Manhattan, you are the heart of New York, America, the entire world. You took her heart as soon as she stepped on your ground over ten years ago.

***

While she was in the restroom, EdwarD ordered another bottle of wine and poured some into her glass. His eyes flew across the dining room and landed on her

10

physique. When she moves, electricity is produced. You absorb all the vibrations coming your way and you want more. EdwarD can feel this sensation, because he is an average man who loves breasts, women's behinds, sex and pretty much all that is in it. He always wanted her, wanted her for his kind of fun. She was open-minded and very playful. What more could he ask for?

She is wearing a tight white dress up to her knees. Her cleavage is very revealing in order to show her fake large breasts pushed up by a Victoria's Secret bra with extra padding. The high-heeled black boots up to her knees make her long legs appear even longer. She is not wearing gloves anymore, she is different now or at least she wanted to be. As she sits next to him at the table, he passes her a filled wine glass.

- *Thank you.* (She took a sip from the glass.) *Tonight many memories came back. When I got your email, I was very confused. I was not sure how uncomfortable our meeting would be. I have to admit that I still feel good in your company. Thank you very much for giving me this special night.*

EDWARD - I will give you something more. (Edward's smile had the power to melt you like a snowflake in a hot oven.) I am sure there is at least something left after I take off that bra.

- *You know how much I love it when you take everything off of me. And I mean everything.* (When she winked, it looked like a butterfly blew a kiss to you.)

EDWARD - We have so much to catch up on. So, how is your business going or whatever else brings you all that money? Every time when I filed for taxes, it amazed me how much money I made by doing nothing. (He chuckled.)

- Good enough not to talk about it. This wine tastes so light, but it is hitting me too fast. It reminds me of you, my love, EdwarD. You started easy on me, ended up taking my entire heart, and then everything else.

EDWARD - When you purchase somebody's body, you get heart for gratis.

- I forgot how romantic you can be. I love you! Now, that is romantic.

EDWARD - You do?

- Yes, I do. I love you, EdwarD as much as before, if not even more.

EDWARD - Listen, you know I am not in love with you. I never was and I never will be. I am sorry, BarbiE. I am not playing with you nor giving you fake hope. You know what I want and what I can give to you, the same as before. No obligations, no worries.

- Tonight I had enough wine. Excuse me. I have no time to waste. (She was about to get up and leave.)

EDWARD - Hold on! Wait! Let me explain myself.

- EdwarD, I do understand very well what you have to say. To make it clear to you: Things are different now!

EDWARD - What is different? You have some money, which is good, but the past will never be changed. You are a former prostitute and you will always carry that title. If we would take our relationship for a long run, sooner or later your past would come up to the surface and both of us would get hurt.

- There is not one thing that cannot be controlled. Control is just a feeling and you can make the decision to believe that you keep something under control or not. The past is no different.

EDWARD - Listen, I don't know everything about you and what I do know, is not something that is easy to deal with. We were a few years apart and I missed you. You are somebody to me. No one that I know has a heart as good as yours. You are strong and capable of more things than I am. Believe it or not, in my eyes, you are a clean woman. It is just that I turned my life in a different direction. Wrong direction maybe, but different! My marriage is not what I want it to be. My wife gave me everything that you never could, but she can never give me what you can.

- You said enough already. I cannot leave this place, despite how much I want to, because we are on a boat, but at least I can sit at a different table. Do not come close to me.

At the bar, she found an empty stool and she ordered a bottle of wine and started drinking from it. The wine was leaking from her mouth and found a way to make decorations on her white dress, but she didn't care. The boat was not stable, and she was even less firm.

***

Passengers are leaving the boat. Manhattan is waiting to offer a new experience to each person. She is laughing so unusually that you can hear the pain coming out before the laughter. EdwarD approached her and took her in his arms like he did years ago. She didn't hesitate to hold him back.

The hotel room previously booked did not end up empty. The two of them were inside. EdwarD was trying to relax his arms. When a drunken woman gives you oral sex while you are driving to a hotel, talks to every person on the way, and spends more time in your arms than on her feet, you get a little bit exhausted. If the woman is attractive, however, you don't mind as much.

The hotel room looks heavenly. White color is everywhere. White carpet, white sheets on the king size bed, white curtains and a white sofa at the edge of the bed are blending in with the white walls. They are in the bed. Bodies are covered with clothes and sheets, but every part of the heart is naked, almost.

- EdwarD, why didn't you want me? You rejected me so many times.

EDWARD - We'll talk when you become sober. Sleep now.

- Why didn't you take my clothes off? Now, I am not good enough to be naked for you?

EDWARD - As I said, sleep and we'll talk tomorrow.

- No! No! And no! I am not going to listen. Tell me, why didn't you want me? Why? Why not?!

EDWARD - You are not good enough for me, that's why.

- I see. Who is good enough for you, then?

EDWARD - Definitely not a prostitute! You have no class, education or the same desires for the future. BarbiE, I don't want to hurt your feelings, but don't ask me to be honest if you can't handle it.

- OK. You can go now.

EDWARD - Go where? I'll stay with you tonight.

- Go wherever you want, just stay away from me.

EDWARD - Is that what you really want?

- Yes, EdwarD. I don't need you, I never did.

She turned on her side and became silent. EdwarD left the room. In the morning, she woke up with a headache and heartache. Both will go away shortly.

In December, it is very cold in Manhattan. Tall buildings tried to keep her warm, but she didn't realize it. A long time ago, she stopped caring what is going on around her, unless something is in her way. She entered Grand Central with the still fresh memories of EdwarD. He is still a romantic guy. He probably paid a lot of money for the room. Why did she still love him so much?

More than an hour later, she arrived in White Plains. Her car was covered with snow. Saturdays are good to go out, because when you come back on Sunday, you don't need to worry about a parking meter. The roads were clean, so driving upstate was not a difficult task. By the time she reached The Doll House, she had plenty time to get ready for work. Sundays are slow, but still work must go on.

***

She is snuggling on her bed with her thoughts lying down next to her. Her red shirt matches her blood-shot eyes and her hair, folded in a bun, is much like her crumpled soul.

Standing next to the coffee table, DaxoN is staring at her. He is radiating blue color: blue eyes, blue tight t-shirt and blue jeans. She is not even acknowledging his appearance.

DAXON - Boss, you didn't even realize that I am here. I came a little bit earlier than usual. What's wrong with you?

- I went out with EdwarD last night. By the way, I have no idea what was going on last night. You took care of everything, right?

DAXON - I wasn't here. I needed some time to clear my head. I am sure SamanthA handled everything. How is EdwarD?

- As always. Love is like milk. When you taste milk and if it is sour, with time, it will become only more sour.

DAXON - Why did you go to see him?

- Because I thought that now I might be good enough for him. Now I have a successful business. I was dressed like a lady and acted like one for a few hours until I got drunk. But, I will never be different in his eyes.

DAXON - Do you regret seeing him?

- No, it is not good to carry around the feeling of regret. Maybe this time, I have realized that he will never be mine.

DAXON - Why do you want him so bad? Why do you have such deep feelings for him?

- EdwarD knows how to speak and act. He will offend you in such a sweet way, that you will wish for more. He was always there for me. He never told me what I wanted to hear, he was always straight forward. I knew what he wanted from me and what I would be able to get from him, but I still had stupid hope. EdwarD is an honest man, who is

16

everything that I am not. When he was getting married, I blamed myself, because I was not good enough for him. I just love him and out of love, I will always find an excuse for his actions.

DAXON - I would listen more about your issues, but you were not there for me when I needed you, so it is "pay-back" time. (He laughed.)

- I am so sorry, DaxoN. I should have given you a shoulder to cry on, but I did not. It will never happen again. I promise.

DAXON - I know you didn't think my situation was serious, and I know you wanted to toughen me up. Listen; there is a reason why I came earlier tonight. I need to tell you something.

- Yeah, what?

DAXON - Do you remember when your cousin DevY died in the accident?

- Yes, of course, why?

DAXON - The case is open again. The house got sold again and while new owners were remodeling it, they found some new evidence that could help find the murderer.

- I did not even know that you were still following that story. I thought you stopped being a private investigator when you started working for me. Anyway, which kind of new clues did they find?

DAXON - I will let you know as soon as I find out something new. I only follow this case because he is your cousin, and it is a shame that a good man like him ended up the way he did.

She said nothing back; her opinion is reserved only for her Facebook friends. Time for a new post!

POST "RANDOM THOUGHTS" 59: *Does anybody have some time for me? I just want to talk to somebody. I need someone to listen and that is the best thing that I can get right now. I do not deserve help or advice. I know that I am nobody and that I didn't deserve anything good. Maybe, just maybe, someone might be interested to hear what one sinner thinks. Well, it is everybody's choice to listen or not, but I will talk anyway.*

This morning, I just feel empty and my tears are heavy on my cheeks. I do not have a big good side inside myself, because my bad side needed more space to develop and I think it went out of control. I do not regret, for what? You are not going to judge me, because you do not know me. You are just too busy looking at amazing lives getting more successful. I am not upset, it is OK. If I do not love myself, how can I expect that from you? I have no reason to even like myself; I never did anything good for myself anyway.

It bothers me so much to see a beautiful woman becoming successful in her life, so confident and arrogant, and at the end, she gets everything that she wanted. Also, she acquires everything that I wished with all my heart to have. How can all that go together? Why do those kinds of women exist? Are they here to fill up ugly and miserable women, like me, with more hate and self-pity? Well, I will be on the side, waiting for their failure, which eventually must come, so I can get a little bit of happiness, too.

Oh, how much I miss some people. How much I wish to have them or somebody special next to me, so I can receive just one short hug. I forgot how love smells. I do not remember how an honest laugh sounds, or how eyes filled with love look like. When did unconditional love and honesty die; the day I left my family?!

Why God don't you change something? Stop being so slow, please! There are rules created by you and who does not respect them deserves to be punished. See, it is that simple. You punish me for every sin, no matter how small it is. Stupid people like me do not understand anything in an easy way, so it would be nice if I could get a slow and detailed explanation about why good people need to suffer? Why kids have to be sexually abused? Why politicians sit down together and over a glass of expensive drink, try to fix their country, meanwhile they have sent so many people to fight until they lose their lives? Why don't those politicians send their own daughters and sons to war? Actually, is the war really necessary? Why do illnesses take away kids' lives? Why are women still suppressed and not appreciated enough?

Why would you bother with this? No one will care for others as long as money exists. At the end, who am I to care for these issues?

I hate to feel powerless, sad and miserable, but I love the feeling of hate. I need the hate to push me through another night, day or maybe a year. Hate might not be stronger than love, but for sure, it is a faster push through life.

CHAPTER 3

PAST 1

A nineteen year-old girl entered illegally into the United States of America through Mexico. She came to Mexico with a fake visa and there, she paid a large amount of money for a false American passport. As part of a plan, she was accompanied by two girls with real American passports. Without any problems, they all passed inspection on the border between Mexico and Texas in a black Mercedes with American plates. All three girls were very attractive, so the inspection department paid more attention to their half-naked bodies than to their passport qualities.

The two American girls left her in Florida and from there, she traveled on a few buses to come to NYC. Everything was going according to plan.

One suitcase, a head full of plans, and a broken heart were the only treasures she owned. After sleeping in buses for a few days, she looked pretty messy. It wasn't hard to find a public library where she was able to use the Internet. With only less than a hundred dollars left in her pocket, she booked a bed in a hostel in Brooklyn. The cost of a bed was a luxurious twenty-dollars plus taxes for one night. However, she appreciated the shower and the clean bed.

Early in the morning, she visited many restaurants hoping to get employment. The first day she did not have luck. The second and third were no different. They did not have a waitress position open or any other kind of job for a girl without a resume and experience. The fourth day, she only had enough money to reach the city and she knew that she would not be able to buy a subway ticket back to the hostel or to pay for a bed. But after all, it was her lucky day; she finally got a job. In Midtown Manhattan, a restaurant needed a dishwasher immediately, so she ended up washing dishes and cleaning the kitchen. The leftover food from the plates finished in her mouth instead of the trash can. It was nice to be able to have a decent meal for the first time in many weeks. When the sixteen hour shift ended, she was tired, but proud of herself. The boss paid her eighty dollars and arranged a work schedule for her. The first week, she slept in the subway every night because she didn't have the money to afford anything else. After working all day long, she was even too tired to carry her suitcase around. Summer nights in Manhattan tended to get very humid which made her even more exhausted. The little money that she made in the restaurant had to be saved. Subways were comfortable enough for getting a few hours of rest and safer at night than any outside environment. Also, she loved to look through the window once the subway reached the Bronx or Brooklyn.

At work, she wore a uniform after she washed her body in the bathroom. In the kitchen, she worked with three Mexicans. One dishwasher boy, named PedrO, spent a lot of time with her. He was in his early thirties, short, muscular and bald. One of PedrO's roommates moved out so he had one spot on the floor available. A few days later, she moved in with him and his six other roommates in a studio apartment. One weekly paycheck was enough to pay her monthly rent and she still had some money left. Finally, she was sleeping in a non-moving bed. All eight roommates had a different schedule, so most of the time, there was enough space on the floor for sleeping. The bathroom was also easily accessible.

Two months later, she got a promotion; she became a waitress. Money was going out from her hands in the same direction as before. Every other paycheck was on the way to her country for her family. The rest of the money was for rent, savings and some clothes.

Being a waitress in NYC was considered a very well paid job. She was a nice-looking young girl with a strong accent who knew how to serve and please people. The tips were so high, that she was able to send double the amount of money back home.

One day a week she had off which she used to finally start exploring the city. Ten months later, she wanted to change her place of living, so she did some research online. Out of curiosity, she made an appointment for an interview with a family who were seeking a nanny for their two precious children. She got the job; she became the live-in nanny.

***

Central Park would brighten when she would run around with the seven-year old twin boys. The job paid her almost eight-hundred dollars per week and she had her own bedroom for the first time in her life. The kids were very spoiled and they didn't listen to anybody, but she was able to manage them for the sake of money.

Almost one year later, she needed a change and she needed to act fast. Her family wanted to move to the US. In order to make that happen, she had to fix her own immigration status first. How do you get a green card when you don't know anybody who might help or give advice? Hours and hours she spent on the Internet researching ways of getting a green card. For her problem, there was only one solution: marriage.

Time was running and patience was never her strong characteristic. The "Craigslist" web site contained almost everything that a person could ask for, so why wouldn't she be able to find a husband there? Yes, she met her husband on Craigslist. Not that many people replied (she was on the bottom compared to other gals), but one man was enough to supply her with a green card. She posted sexy photos taken by the camera on her prepaid cellphone in the hopes that somebody would have a big enough sexual desire, at least, to marry her. Sex was her only strong card which she knew very well. Some girls looking for green cards had money to offer and some had enough time on their hands to choose. She had none of those, but still she got lucky.

He was in his early sixties, she was twenty. After a few dates, she learned that he was the nicest man on this planet. He promised to fix her papers if she worked for him as a housekeeper, for free, until her documents arrived. As a good hearted man, he hated to see young women giving up their dignity in the name of a green card. This gentleman was an angel sent by God in her life, until she married him.

The wedding reception was in his house. One of his friends was a judge who married them. Altogether, twenty people were present, including his two close friends who were medical doctors.

The first night he raped her, but she did not mind, for she was raped many times before. His old and spongy hands were fast and rough. His breath was rotten, because of all of the cavities that he had on the few real teeth left in his mouth. He was bald with a long beard, sharp as a knife. She took his roughness without complaining. Encounters were always short, but never pleasant. She hated old men, but her love for a green card was stronger.

The marriage lasted the entire year. They had their bad days and that is the only thing they had, besides the nice house, expensive car and a lot of money. She carried the hope of getting her green card and who knows what he carried in this marriage, definitely some kind of mental disease.

Time passed, the abuse did not. Screaming, beating, pushing, and raping she was able to handle, but she could not accept the fact that God gave up on her. Over a lifetime, these things became her reality, the only kind she ever knew.

She cooked and cleaned the house naked. He was turned on by her nudity. When it came to feeding her body, he did not allow her to eat proper meals. According to him, chubby women do not deserve to live. Her foods were rare diet meals. Her only energy source was the hope that soon she will get a chance to have an honest hardworking life devoted to benefit her family, not herself. She never dared to consider her own needs.

Time did not wait, so after almost a year of marriage, she dared to ask him if she received any papers from immigration.

DEVY - Papers, hugh? You fucking illegal immigrants only think about that! Let me explain something to you.

Now, while I am talking to you, you are going to suck my dick! If you don't do it, you're going to jail, and even American prisoners don't adore illegal immigrants. Unzip my jeans, my dear Stinky ButterflY; be useful for once in this marriage.

- *Please, tell me when I will get them. I did everything that we agreed, I never complained, I was patient, isn't it my turn now?*

DEVY - Yes, it is your turn to be beaten in the kidneys again!

It took her two moves to have his dick in her mouth. The hooker career can be very useful in variable situations, such as these. He was making pleasant noises and his mood got brighter.

DEVY - This is America, we have everything and we don't like to share. Most of our success is based on somebody's sweat. Yeah, right there. Like that. Open your mouth more. Ugh! Immigrants are slaves, very colorful ones. Every day when I go to the Federal Plaza, I look forward to making American citizens happy by returning smart immigrants and keeping the losers who will serve America. I can smell if a marriage is false, but even when I know it is real, what a pleasure it is to reject one stinky immigrant. Hold it in your hands and lick my balls. Nice, I don't want to cum yet; I just want to be relaxed. Ahh, you are doing some fine job, my Stinky ButterflY. You immigrants come here with the dreams and high hopes. Why? Who do you think you are? Do we owe you something? You don't belong here. This is not your country and never will be. Oh! Slow down, stupid idiot. Your mother is a woman who gives you birth, and your country is where you are born. You don't leave a mother, just because another woman is prettier and smarter, so don't leave your country just because you want more. I never even submitted your stinky paperwork! You are still illegal and always will be. Suck it now! Don't you dare to stop just because some bad news is flying through your big ears! I think we are a good couple; I can bring you your green card any minute. Make me happy once and you will have the document in your hands. That is enough for now. Go ahead and clean my feet, my toe nails are a little bit long.

- You made a deal with me. It was supposed to be one year...

A hand slapping a bony face is not a quiet noise. Her kidneys are receiving his foot prints and she is crying not only because of the physical pain, but for the fact that she will not get what she needs: a green card. It represented the opportunity to make her family finally happy.

***

The house is located in Long Island, NY. You cannot pass by and not turn your head a couple of times. It is as big as a large cathedral, grey and white colors are dancing a smooth ballet on the house's walls. What a spectacle! More than forty kinds of flowers, weird-shaped trees and four water fountains guard this modern-style palace. You can smell the beauty.

The owner, DevY, is a much respected American citizen who proved to the nation that he is the angel guardian of this part of the Earth. After his father's death, he received the amount of eight-million dollars. As a good raised son should do, he took care of his

26

mother and his sick older brother. It was a big responsibility for a twenty-year-old male. Unfortunately, his brother burned himself to death one year later, at the age of twenty-two. The mother passed away from cardiac arrest two years later.

DevY pushed himself through school with his hard work in the Microsoft Company. He also graduated with an Immigration law degree to make some changes in the government system. He never had limits in anything. Deeply involved in politics and humanitarian work, soon he became a very well-known and respected man. He married his cleaning lady and they were a happy couple for many years. They did not have any biological kids, but they adopted seven of them. All of them have different origins. After the seventh child was adopted, DevY asked for a divorce. Ten years of marriage were thrown away without explanation. He bought a ten bedroom house in Beverly Hills and his ex-wife moved there with seven children. At the age of thirty-two, he was a father and a divorced man. Every month, all the bills were paid. Even later on after his death, his ex-wife never missed anything.

Eight-million of inherited dollars did not help him become successful. He donated the money to political campaigns and a charity for helping immigrants. A few months later, he became the leader of the same charity company.

Immigration (mostly in the Federal Plaza), politics and humanitarian work occupied his time and his mind. In his rare free time, he did some small jobs for Microsoft. Occasionally, he paid restaurants across Manhattan to serve buffet food to immigrants, illegal and legal. He was present each time.

When he reached his sixties, he did not retire from any job. To everybody's surprise, he got married once again, but no one was surprised to find out that his new bride was an immigrant. The poor girl was born with some kind of syndrome, but he did not mind at all. Eventually, he was slowing down his work, just to be with her. She was afraid of people. DevY arranged for two doctors to come and visit almost every week. The house had one room which served as a hospital room.

The neighbors, immigrants and citizens were all lucky to have DevY to take care of them, including his new sick wife, which he called "Beautiful Butterfly".

The world is full of sneaky people. DevY was just one of many who belonged in this category. Even though he was seen as a true angel, the reality proved differently.

***

At the age of three, he was introduced to computers. Knowledge of reading and math found a shortcut to his brain through computer learning games. School work and the Internet were his best and only friends until the age of fifteen. Through his entire education, he was called a "freaky nerd". All the money that his family had, could not buy him a friend. All of his classmates, during his private education located in Manhattan, were wealthy. Having girlfriends was out of consideration. DevY's mother was obsessed with her two sons; they were the center of her existence, so it had to be the other way around, too. His father was a hard-working man, always on the go across the world, taking care of his international real estate business and humanitarian work for the improvement of poor and forgotten people. The mother was a lonely housewife focused on protecting her sons from others.

DevY loved to watch adult movies, all kinds. The mother knew what was going on; she always checked the browsing history on their computer, while her sons were at school. Eventually, the time came when he became his own mother's lover. Now she had two sons to please her. The father's weak heart (he already had three surgeries related to his heart problems) was not able to handle the discovery of the mother with their two sons in bed. The boys did not look happy, but the mother looked pleased. After the father fell down on an expensive rug in his master bedroom, he dropped a few tears down his cheek. Both boys were afraid of the outside world, so the mother continued to have control even when they became adults. DevY's brother found his solution: he burned himself in the same master bedroom where his father passed away. The mother changed a lot after that, now she had more control over DevY. Many times, she went to work with him to keep an eye on her beloved child.

One evening, the cleaning lady came early to clean the office where DevY worked on his humanitarian projects. She was such a sexy uneducated woman, but a man does not care as long as his dick sings happy. That same night, they had sex and he enjoyed it. Somebody else besides his mother was kissing him, and he loved it.

That night, he attended the free buffet dinner for immigrants that he organized. When he was in the kitchen with his chef, who was paid way more than his skills were worth, DevY urinated only in a few dishes (pasta sauce, chicken soup, shrimp cocktail and in salad dressings). Usually, he gave his flavor into all dishes. Immigrants loved attending these parties. The food was delicious and they loved to meet people who were going in the same direction; toward receiving their green cards.

DevY knew he had to get rid of his mother, so he asked for help from a doctor who loved money way more than principles. Four pills were melted in her wine which gave a fruity taste in the mouth. When the mother finished her glass of wine, she finished her life.

The cleaning lady became filthy rich after marrying DevY. Money gave her security, but not happiness. A smile on an orphan's face was wealth for her soul. In less than ten years, she gave a home to seven orphans, all of them immigrants. Teaching English was her talent that seven children benefited from.

If the orphans were Americans, DevY would never leave his wife. How could he explain to her that he hates all immigrants with no reason? He asked her to give him space so he could figure out what he wanted to do with his life. Giving her money was nice marketing for his reputation, even though it was not his desire to secure immigrant orphans.

Politicians always need sponsors and sponsors always need a favor from politicians. If you donate a few million to humanitarian organizations, you get gratitude and those thankful people have no problem to let you lead.

Years and years of loneliness could give you courage for an adventure. Craigslist was the fastest way to find whatever you needed, even if what you needed was a wife. He did not plan to make a good husband, and he would never be able to hurt an American woman, so he chose a desperate illegal immigrant. It took him only a few nice words, a pleasant dinner in his gorgeous house and one promise of giving a green card, to get a hand and ownership of somebody's life.

Marriage can make your dreams come true or make your life hell. For DevY's new wife, the life was not hell, it was way worse. He locked her in the house and for one year, she never felt the outside air on her skin. Security devices were all over the house and DevY himself had a very good ability to control; at least his mom gave him something useful.

In the beginning, his new wife was full of escape plans, but all attempts ended devastatingly for her body, especially her kidneys. For almost a year, she was in the worst imaginable jail. Two well-respected doctors visited her and DevY almost every week to assess her health. The hospital room was located in the basement and it was used for making porn movies. DevY was the producer, his wife and the doctors were actors. She played a sick woman being sexually abused in her hospital bedroom. Many times, all three men had beaten her up just for fun.

DevY hired a landscaping agency to take care of his land, but his wife was responsible for the house and him. She was such a strong women, she took every pain and swallowed it. The picture of a green card covered the main screen in her brain.

In that period of time, her family received only a few letters, some of them contained a few stolen bills, which she sneaked into his huge pile of mail. His secretary mailed them all without asking questions. Before she got married, she sent a nice amount of money, but she never imagined that it would take almost a year to hear from USCIS (U.S. Citizenship and Immigration Services).

- My God, I am begging you for help. Do something, anything, just make a change. Where am I heading to? What is in front of me? How is my family? Do they still remember me? Does my little baby sister know my face? Why did You forget me? Is this what You want for me? Are You happy to see me in pain? When is it going to be enough for You, because I have had enough a long time ago? Make my family not need me and I will end my existence. Can You at least do that for me? Just that and forget everything else. But, at the end, I know You will not do anything for me. Why would You? Who am I to You? You know what? Just carry on and don't pay attention to me. That is what You are really good at! Amen.

That was her shower prayer, the only place where she had a few moments alone. Another half a year passed by and nothing very different happened. The same three high-classed men played with her and the same hope stayed in her heart. Patience! How important that talent is. You have to believe! She forgot about that in an honest way. Prayers stopped coming from the mouth, but she continued praying with her actions. She just didn't know it.

Not for one second did God give up on her. It just was not the right time to make huge changes. He had to wait according to His clock, not hers or yours. She cared the most about her family and God took care of them. God protects what is important to you without notice. He is not a "show-off".

One of the two doctors had to do some new experiments related to his new cream. He was really good at inventing, and now it was time for the development of something very unique: a cream that could completely renew skin in just a few minutes. In his office, he had people for testing. The cream recovered skin from burns, cuts and even sun damage. Would this cream be able to cure skin that was damaged with an alkaline liquid? Today he will find out after doing an experiment on DevY's wife.

It took all three of them to restrain her on a chair. The doctor prepared beakers filled with sodium hydroxide. The first tip of her finger was held inside the glass for less than one second. The second time, he held it for five seconds, enough time to burn the deep tissue. The ten tips of her fingers were destroyed; each of them in a different way. Some of them were burned up to the bones and on others, just the first few layers of skin. What a pain! As the result, the cream was not able to restore the skin from alkaline damage. After much disappointment, sex comes like a medicine. The three men loved her way of crying, it turned them on above their own limits. She looked so fragile and it looked like she could be broken with one wrong move, but they didn't mind. It was worth it.

After an amazing pleasure, all three of them left the room to have beer while watching CNN news. Both of the doctors left shortly after that. Only DevY was left with the bottle of expensive wine.

***

Eyes so peaceful and relaxed, hair falling down her bony back, legs and arms spread apart. Lying down

33

on her stomach never felt so comfortable. The pain! Not only in her fingers, but all over her body! It was not a regular pain, it felt strong and sharp. Vibrating waves were going through every atom of her body. This kind of pain cleans you up. Mental strength takes over the body. Enough was enough! Anger took its place. At that moment, the agony gave her strength to go beyond the human pain threshold.

DEVY - Stinky ButterflY, where are you? I am calling you and you are not showing up. I guess somebody needs some bones broken! Yes! Not one bone is broken in your ugly body and you need that! Get over here! I will find you and you cannot escape, so don't make me even angrier! Come here now and I promise to break only your arm and nothing else! Come here! Come here, you fucking useless immigrant!...Fuck!!! Oh God!!!!!

The minute DevY opened the hospital room door, she threw alkaline liquid in his face. He fell on the floor and took off his shirt to try to wipe it off. In the room were tape, scissors, a knife, a belt, candles and many other things that DevY and his friends used to play with. Many times, she was taped to the bed while they let the candles drip on her body.

This time, DevY was taped to the bed. He looked like a strong man, but as soon as he tasted some pain, he became weak and scared. Her bones worked in harmony. It took her a few minutes to position his old body in the bed. He cried like a bitch! She wanted to play with him the same way she played with her own father in his last moments, but this time, there was no time to waste.

- Alright American Citizen DevY, after a year, it is my turn to take over! We immigrants appreciate time and we are always in a rush to make a successful life! We do not come here to take something from you; we come to make something for ourselves and you. We love to share; we always take care of ones less fortunate because we never forget who we were and who we want to be. Hard work is our teacher and our egos get crushed, but never killed.

Snip! She cut his dick off with the scissors, just like Lorena Bobbitt from Manassas did with a knife. DevY lost his voice after ten minutes of screaming. Who would say that scissors can cut meat like a paper? Who would say that a victim stops being a victim overnight?

- Where is your voice, my honey? Do you want me to suck your dick now? Oops, you don't have one. You are bleeding, let me warm up a candle and put it on your tiny cut between your legs. You see, after you break so many dreams, somebody will come along and not break your dream, but break you.

She realized that DevY was calm, almost gone. Maybe he was dead or maybe not. Why did he have to be so weak? It was her turn to make him suffer and God protected him.

The plan had to be made. It was eleven o'clock at night and she had to hurry. Before doing something important, a person has to do two things to be ready: Wash your body and get some sleep. There was no time for sleeping, but a shower sounded reasonable. She rinsed her fingers over and over, hoping that not only would the alkaline disappear, but this year of her life would down the drain, too. The pain was masked with anxiety and her clean body was clothed with black jeans and a tight shirt with long black sleeves. She had a black jacket on, too. The gloves secured the pieces of gauze on each of her fingers. One bag was filled with some clothes and another bag with the money from DevY's office drawer. The wooden desk was easily broken, so what was the point of locking the drawer in it? He never thought about that. Over tens of thousands of dollars should be helpful until she upgrades her plan. As a bonus, in the drawer, was an envelope with her fake driver's license, fake passport and a properly filled petition I-485 for her green card. In the basement, she found her old black shoes. She was ready to go to the outside world of America!

She taped the smoke alarms as best as she could to prevent the smoke being detected. Salt was spread around the hospital room, which soon became a fire place. Salt likes the fire. The bar became empty. Alcohol was spread around the house along with oil. While DevY's body was in the fire, he woke up in pain and he smelled his own skin burning, realizing that his punishment finally came. A few seconds later, the knife went deep into his neck.

The broken window activated the security alarm and it was a push for her to run faster. The skinny, tall woman with two bags, walked down the street. Police, fire trucks and an ambulance were all singing at once, not realizing that they are too late; almost one year too late. For the immigrant, they seem to be forever late, while for the citizen, they are only moments late. Regardless, they are too late.

As soon as she arrived on a busier street, a cab pulled over to pick her up. Finally, God's clock and her clock showed the same time.

CHAPTER 4

She was laying down on top of her king size bed in her studio apartment while chatting on the phone with MarrY.

- Hey MarrY! May I come over to have a cup of tea with you?

MARRY - Well, in my age, I'm hardly able to hold the phone in my hand, so I don't even dare to think about taking more than a few steps at once. I'll be home so you are more than welcome to come.

- Oh, please MarrY. You are able to run a marathon if you want. Have you gone to church lately?

MARRY - Yes, I was there last Sunday and I didn't see you. How come you didn't have time for God?

- On Saturday night I went out and I came home Sunday. I did not have such a peaceful weekend. I will be in your house in less than an hour. Do you need anything from the store?

MARRY - Tea would be nice, I don't have any left. Listen, while you are already shopping, get some red nail polish.

- Done deal. See you soon, my beautiful MarrY.

She put her cell phone in her purse, took the car keys and left The Doll House. She drove fifteen minutes north, so she could purchase the red nail polish. MarrY is the most important woman in the US to her. They met a few years ago in church and since then, the stores sold a lot of tea.

MarrY's house is located in the middle of nowhere. It takes more than ten minutes to walk to her house from the car parked on the side road. But when you reach the house, you see an amazing picture in front of your eyes. Snow-covered barren flowering trees surround the house. It looks like a private white botanical garden. In this time of the year, everything is hidden under a white cover, but spring is around the corner. The house is way too big for one person, but cozy enough for a family of four. After losing both kids and her husband, MarrY devoted her life to nature and God. She continued to take care of the farm and she tried to stop being angry towards Him. Every Sunday, she walked two miles to church just to get an answer. One Sunday, she was facing another kind of loss and a young blonde woman came in her life from nowhere and fixed the problem. That day, MarrY found another person who had the same issues with God. Both of them needed each other for sharing their painful stories.

When she arrived at MarrY's house, she laid the bags on her table and embraced her in a loving hug. MarrY prepared tea and served it with a plate of cookies.

MARRY - Red nail polish is symbol of power. Not every woman can handle this color. (Marry exclaimed the statement while she was admiring her old hands.)

- *Okay, I know you are powerful and strong.* (She said it in a teasing voice.) *Listen, I went out with EdwarD.*

MARRY - Why, you stupid woman? (MarrY even raised her hands to heaven so she could understand better why people make mistake after mistake.)

- *EdwarD e-mailed me few days ago and he wrote down the address and the time of the meeting. I was very happy to hear from him after a few years. We met in Manhattan on a cruise. Everything was romantic and there was nothing to discuss from his side. He just wanted to have sex. Probably things with his wife are not blooming. The problem is that I still feel that I owe him a lot.*

MARRY - I know you have a past with him and he did many things for you, but you were there for him, too. He gave you what he wanted to give you. He took from you what he wanted to take. You took what was given to you and you gave him what he asked from you. So, how can you possibly think that you owe something to him?

- He loved me and no other man ever did.

MARRY - He did not love you. When a man loves a woman, he swims the ocean for her. When a man is in love, he doesn't think, he just follows her. EdwarD had a million excuses not to be with you.

- He understood me. He listened to all my stories and he knows almost my entire life. He gave me money when I needed it and he is the reason why I do not wear gloves anymore. He was the one who kissed my tears... (MarrY cut her off.)

MARRY - You have to let go of the past. EdwarD did some nice things for you, but he hurt you way more. He knew that you were in love with him, yet he married another woman who is everything that you are not. I am not talking from his point of view. I don't care how educated she is or even if she is a virgin. You have a heart. You suffered too much and you never turned your back on people that needed you. I see what you do for people that you never even met and especially how loyal you are to your family. By the way, how are they?

- I called them this morning and my brother is sick more than ever before. The cancer is way too strong. I sent them some money and that is all I can do from here. I cannot go there, so I have to let God punish me again by taking my brother away.

MARRY - I hope he'll get better soon. Your stepmother must appreciate all the help she gets from you.

- I feel it is never enough. There is another thing that I want to talk to you about. I live in fear every day. I have to let the business down.

MARRY - Why? Why would you do something like that? (Marry poured more tea in her cup, just to steal a few seconds to absorb the shocking news.)

- DaxoN, the guy who works for me...

MARRY - The investigator?

- Yes. He is after me. I feel it. He is in love with one of the clients and it is not good between them, so DaxoN does not care about The Doll House anymore. He told me that the case about DevY's death is open again.

MARRY - I don't understand why you hired an investigator in the first place.

- I wanted to know what the police know. I thought that I would be able to get my green card through some other way. Now I know that the police looked for me all these years and they will not stop until they get me.

MARRY - You can always defend yourself. You killed him in "self-defense".

- How do I prove it? You know that he is the angel in people's eyes. I just have to hide again until DaxoN loses track of me. I saved money and this time, I should be financially stable enough for a longer period than last time.

MARRY - Which last time? You've had so many new beginnings already. (Marry had to let at least one smile escape.)

- You know what I mean. When I escaped from DevY, it was the beginning of a new kind of hell. And when EdwarD kicked me out of his life, it was even worse. This time it should be different. I have you, right?

MARRY - Yes, you do. I feel sorry for you if I am the best thing in your life right now.

- Stop it, MarrY! Well anyway, I am planning to move in with you for a while.

MARRY - It would be my pleasure. These flowers need more attention and the farm needs a lot of strength. (She laughed.) You know I'm kidding. I don't need anything from you. I will do whatever I can to help you.

- You know I will help you as much as I can. I just need some time to be in peace so that my mind can be cleared up.

Hours flew so fast, the plan was on; the two women will stick together for the benefit of one. That is what friendship is about!

CHAPTER 5

The snowy days were cold, white, and emotional. The Doll House was not busy, but enough of a profit was made. MarrY was full of support as always. DaxoN was in anticipation, waiting to see the masked Phantom of the Opera. SamanthA was in charge of the business. EdwarD was a mystery as he was for the last few years, and she was living in a mess as always.

POST "RANDOM THOUGHTS" 60: *Oh, my dear, the New Year is in front of me and you. Not even the snow is the same. Finally, it should be a time for new ideas, plans, and goals for exciting and different achievements. Every year, I start them and I end up at the same beginning twelve months later. What am I doing wrong? Probably many things, but I have such a good excuse for my actions. I tried to make every step of my life perfect and it did not work that way. I could not let go. I needed some things to be done immediately, so if it could not be done in a nice way, it was done in the only possible way in that moment. You do understand me, right?*

Now it is a holiday season and I believe I have done enough good deeds for others. Look at me, sitting in the stinky corner of my room. Years ago, I used to believe that I could make a living by working jobs approved by moral standards; waitress, nanny, cleaning lady and care giver. The kids have had a home, their own room, parents, a real Christmas tree and of course, many presents under the tree itself. I was amazed to see all those beautiful toys, clothes, art supplies and so much more. One thing I have never seen though was excitement on the child's face. How sad is it to kill that feeling? I would love to say to every parent, "If you love your child, never give them everything!"

I am not sure if I should ask you these questions, but I do not have anyone else to talk to. Did you ever feel that you deserve more than you have? Did you do more for others than for yourself? There are people in your life that you live for. They always come before you and for them, you do not think twice; you have no limits when it comes to their well-being. The love for them will make you strong and be there to give you a push when you need it, but also that same love will destroy you. You will forget that you have somebody else to take care of: you. Do not worry, you and I do not need our own happiness to live; we live from happiness of our loved ones. At least that is what keeps me one step away from hurting myself.

The New Year will be here in less than four days, so there is some room left for acting stupid. But of course, she believed that the next year, she will not do anything like that.

She logged out of her Facebook and opened her email. It was time for something unwise, but exciting.

From: green.card@hotmail.com
To: edward.NYC@gmail.com
Subject: *Happy New Year*

EdwarD, I have not heard from you since dinner. I lied to you when I said that I did not need you. Please, take some time to think about me. I asked Santa to give me an email from you, but I guess I was a naughty girl, so I did not get it. Maybe I can start the New Year by reading an email from you. Make me happy, please.

I wrote a poem for you...

Amusement

Still living in an amusement,
tear by tear I will move on,
tear by tear, I will forget what through I went.

Along the way this is what I meant;
suffer and suffer until I get tougher.
And I had my promises to be kept,
never you to be sent.

What to do with you?
You do not want me, you don't,
but you are the only man I want.

Living in an amusement
gives me strength.
Do you know my love for you has no length?

All feelings are on one side,
only my heart took a ride.

Amusement is such a nice place,
there I see your face,
day and night,
you are always in my sight.

Amusement, keep me inside,
too many things I tried.
For you I lost my pride.
Still, I am not yours, not even on the side.

You always got everything, lost nothing.
I need you to know something:
without you it is hard breathing.

P.S. I love you so much, EdwarD. You are my angel. I just
love you for what you have done for me. I love you.

CHAPTER 6

Snowflakes are controlled by the wind which makes them dance around The Doll House. It is another cold winter night. She is wearing her black leggings and an oversized black sweater. Her studio apartment is warm, her heart is frozen. The dark roots of her hair are showing and the darkness of her soul is putting her brain in the shade. Her face is pale. Wrinkles under her eyes are getting deeper by the second. Her depression is getting stronger than ever before.

Should I come out and help her? I know I can guide her toward fulfilling her purpose in this life, even though I don't see it yet. For more than thirty years, I have been waiting and I can wait even longer. I will give her another chance to deal with her problems alone.

Her little brother died today. After all these years of fighting cancer, he finally became exhausted. Her little sister and stepmother are devastated, and for the first time, there is nothing that she can do to help them. The fourteen-year-old boy moved in with God today. She never saw him, but she had a hope to meet him. Now, even the hope is gone.

Tomorrow is New Year's Day, so her business is closed tonight. Last night, the customers and the workers of The Doll House, exchanged their gifts and wishes through passionate love-making. She was in the studio for the last few days waiting for EdwarD's email, and today, she received an email from her sister. She was hoping for one surprise and received another one informing her of her brother's death.

The door is being unlocked from the outside and she is expecting DaxoN or SamanthA to walk in, for they are the only people with the key to her studio apartment. When her teary red eyes looked toward the door, she saw EdwarD. He was wearing snow boots, dark blue jeans and a light blue winter jacket. His dark brown hair was covered with a few snowflakes. She jumped from her bed like a cheetah and in less than a second, she was hugging his legs. Like a little puppy, she was squeezing him so hard that he almost fell to the side, but the bathroom door was there to give him much needed support.

EWARD - BarbiE girl, a few days ago you kicked me out of the hotel room and tonight, you are giving me more than a warm welcome. Stand up, let me check you out.

After placing his hands under her arms, he helped her to stand up on her feet. Their eyes locked onto each other.

EDWARD - What happened?

- *The cancer won. I will never see him.*

EDWARD - Oh, baby, oh my God!

Even though EdwarD's eyes were filling with tears fast, he didn't let them escape. He put his right arm around her waist and walked her toward her bed. He seated her on the mattress and then he walked back toward the entrance door. He took off his boots and placed them in the kitchen sink, so that the melting snow could drain down. He put his jacket on the coffee table in front of the entrance. He walked toward her slowly, looking around the place. After he sat on the bed, he placed the pillow on his lap and her head on the pillow. They were facing the TV and the Jacuzzi got his attention.

EDWARD - Nice place. It has everything that you need.

- *Well, now it does.*

EDWARD - I own this place, too, right?

- *Yes, you own every piece of my life.*

EDWARD - BarbiE, I read every email and I just didn't know what to write. I knew this is the only property that you put my name on, so I decided to check it out and see if you lived here. It took me hours to find it. In front of this house, is a parked car with a man crying inside. I wanted to leave, because I thought he was the one who lived here or he was your boyfriend, but I decided to ask him for the answers. As soon as he saw me, it seemed like he recognized me. He handed me the keys and told me to go on the other side of the house and take the stairs to the second floor.

- *That must have been DaxoN, because he is the only man who has the keys and he knows what you look like. I did not know he was here tonight. I wonder why he is crying.*

EDWARD - Who is he?

- *One of my workers.*

EDWARD - Did you have sex with him?

- *He is gay, he finds me disgusting.*

EDWARD - I like him already.

- *Shouldn't you be celebrating New Year's?*

EDWARD - I am. (He continued to play with her hair.)

- *Where is your wife?*

EDWARD - MelanY is in Sidney. I was supposed to meet her there last night, but I had to cancel because I got sick and I couldn't travel. My parents are there, too, so there is no one to check on me. They'll have fun without me.

- Did you plan all that, just to be with me?

EDWARD - Kind of, I lied about getting sick, but my original plan was to fly there after my meeting. Yesterday, I was getting ready to go to JFK when I decided to re-read your emails for the millionth time. I just couldn't leave you alone in New York. Your poem is so not true at all. I didn't get what I wanted and just knowing that you suffer because of me, makes me hate myself.

- You can hate yourself; I love you enough for you and me. Thank you for coming. I need you all the time, especially today. If my sister dies too, I will finish myself as well, I swear.

EDWARD - That won't happen, BarbiE. Your brother was fighting all these years. Your stepmom, sister and you made sure he was happy during his short life.

- Oh, please, I was supposed to bring him here and give him the opportunity to take advantage of American medicine. Leukemia could be cured here, I know it. I donated thousands of dollars to help in the cure of American children and in return, God could not save my brother for me or at least make him come here and get help.

EDWARD - We can talk forever about what we could have done differently, but he is with the angels already.

- I am not even sure if heaven or God exists, but I have to believe in it in order to survive day-by-day.

48

EDWARD - We all do. Listen, BarbiE, let's pray together for your little bother, then we will have a few drinks and the New Year will look much more appealing.

- Whatever you want. Open the fridge and in the first drawer, you will find a set of keys. One of them opens the door into the bar on the first floor. Take as many wine bottles as you want, and bring them upstairs. I will light some candles in memory of the little angel.

Edward placed kisses on both of her eyes and then embraced her in a strong hug.

***

The red candles are placed on the floor in front of the big window across the entrance. She had to push the bed to the side, so there was enough space between the bed and the Jacuzzi for praying.

The entrance door opened, and EdwarD and DaxoN walked inside, carrying wine bottles wrapped in EdwarD's jacket.

EDWARD - BarbiE, this man with me is either naturally crazy or sad crazy, either way, he is able to carry twelve wine bottles wrapped in my jacket. Did you know that I can fit two wine bottles in one sleeve?

While he was talking, he and DaxoN placed all the bottles on the coffee table.

- What's the matter, DaxoN? Why are you here tonight?

DAXON - I was hoping that he might come and make a big step, like maybe propose to me or ask me to run away with him. Some situation like in the fairy tales would be nice.

EDWARD - DaxoN, you are dangerously crazy.

- *Oh EdwarD, you have no idea how much he loves his Phantom of the Opera.*

EDWARD - Phantom of the Opera?

DAXON - I am going to cry.

- *DaxoN, didn't you cry enough already?*

DAXON - Boss, you are the biggest crier I know.

EDWARD - You guys are not answering me. And what is going on downstairs? Why is only wine available?

- *Can I answer all those questions another time? Right now I just want to get drunk.*

DAXON - You don't want to talk in front of me?

- *That is part of the reason, too. DaxoN, I do not need to remind you about your clients, especially that one, do I?*

DAXON - Let's start drinking. Let's sit on the bed and watch TV, too.

EDWARD - BarbiE, whatever you say, but eventually I would like to learn where all that money is coming from.

- *I will tell you, soon. In that case, you have a reason to see me again. DaxoN, before we start drinking, EdwarD and I are going to pray. Do you want to join us? We are praying for someone special.*

DAXON - Sure, I'll pray. I thought these candles were for the atmosphere and not for worshiping.

All three of them were sitting on the floor in front of the candles, looking at the snowflakes through the window. Tears are in all their eyes, all for different reasons. None of them wanted to celebrate the New Year under these kinds of circumstances. After praying, she and EdwarD were laying down on the bed, with wine glasses filled to the top. DaxoN planned to make himself comfortable on the bed, too, but EdwarD's look signaled the danger of that step. The empty Jacuzzi became filled with a comforter and a couple pillows, where DaxoN was relaxing while drinking wine directly from the bottle. A few bottles later, all of them were asleep.

I looked at them and wished them a Happy New Year, knowing that happiness will not be part of hers.

CHAPTER 7

In the afternoon of the New Year, she and EdwarD woke up with a hangover. As soon as she opened her eyes, tears were jumping out. She was thinking about her little brother. EdwarD was looking at her with his eyes full of kindness. After a few minutes of silence, he left the bed to take a water bottle from the fridge. On the way back, he paused by the Jacuzzi, which was not only filled with water, but also with pillows and a comforter. A note was taped on the Jacuzzi faucet.

"Boss, I know you are a neat freak, so I did the laundry for you. Thank you guys for being horrible companions. If anyone cares, I am on my way home. Have fun throwing up! And yeah, Happy New Year! - DaxoN"

EDWARD - He didn't do the entire laundry. Come BarbiE; let's clean you up really good.

- DaxoN is crazy, and right now I am not in the mood for your or his jokes.

She covered herself with a comforter, ready to go back to sleep. EdwarD grabbed her feet and pulled her to the edge of the bed. She wasn't objecting.

EDWARD - Are you going to get in the Jacuzzi by yourself or do I have to carry you inside? But then I will know how much you weigh.

- I am skinny and fat enough for you.

EDWARD - I can't judge what I don't feel.

- I am not taking my clothes off.

EDWARD - I didn't ask you to.

- *Okay then.*

She got off of the bed and sat inside the Jacuzzi in her t-shirt and leggings. EdwarD gave out his surprised smile. His black eyes looked at her green ones with surprise.

EDWARD - I missed your playful side.

- *I missed you. Come in.*

He stepped inside with his jeans and black t-shirt. Both of them were sitting in the cool water, on top of the wet comforter, surrounded with wet pillows. Wet eyes were getting dried by the excitement.

EDWARD - BarbiE, let me wash your body.

- *You said that I did not need to take my clothes off.*

EDWARD - You will not. I will take your clothes off.

- *No, please do not play with my head.*

EDWARD - I don't want to play with your head; I want to play with something else.

Slowly, he took off her t-shirt. She stood up in the Jacuzzi and he pulled down her leggings. She didn't have underwear on. He kissed her private place while she was standing up. He stood up and took off his jeans and underwear in one move. Then he took off his shirt. Both of them were standing. He hugged her with his right arm and with his left hand, he was squeezing her bare bottom. He released her after few seconds and then he started exploring her body. He touched her breasts; his hand was slowly sliding down her stomach. Then his finger moved slowly inside her.

Even though it felt good, she pushed his hand away and kneeled in the cool water so her mouth could face his manhood. With one hand, she was massaging his balls and with another hand, she was holding his masculinity while her mouth was sucking on it.

EDWARD - You will make me cum. Slow down, I don't want to yet.

She ignored his warning and she was sucking on it faster and faster, even though she felt pain in her mouth. He pushed her head away and pulled himself out of her mouth. He sat down next to her. They kissed passionately. Then he turned on the jets on the Jacuzzi and sat behind her, so he would be able to position her legs on the edge while the water from the jet was hitting her clitoris. She was trapped between his legs and his arms, and being trapped in this position, did not allow her to push away from the water pressure.

- EdwarD, I cannot hold it any longer…

EDWARD - You don't have to, cum, cum a lot…

And she did. No man can beat the power of the water. She relaxed in his arms, while he was kissing her eyes and her hair.

EDWARD - I told you I will clean you well. But, you are not completely clean yet.

- Oh no, you are not getting my ass.

EDWARD - We'll see.

EdwarD stood up behind her, and then pulled her up and bended her forward, so his masculinity could reach her while he was standing. She was not comfortable taking it from this position, but she did it for him, for she knew how

54

much pleasure he was getting out of it. He sat on the edge of the Jacuzzi and placed her on top of him while her back was turned. He was heavy breathing on her back while she was moving up and down.

***

She woke up feeling disoriented. A few seconds later, she finally settled in reality. It is New Year's Day, EdwarD was gone, her little brother is in heaven, her business has to be closed, the police are after her and she feels weak; not from the alcohol, but from the stress.

Her inbox is empty, which means her sister didn't get a chance to write an email. She must have been busy with organizing the funeral.

She logged into her Facebook account, so she could occupy her mind.

POST "RANDOM THOUGHTS" 61: *What is wrong with me? I know that I have some mental disorder, but it is impossible to find out its name. The entire US lacks so many basic programs. This is such a smart and yet such a stupid country at the same time.*

I feel that something is wrong with me. I do not have money to spend, and of course, I do not have insurance. That means I cannot pay for my medical exam. In this country, you cannot get free anonymous therapy. Why not? Is it more expensive for the country to make programs where people who think something is wrong with them can go and get needed help, or to let people suffer and act according to their illness? When that happens, it is too late for the government to save money. Emergency care, police, and fire fighters have to be paid for their service. And the lost lives need nothing at the end.

The last few weeks, I spent searching for a free psychologist, who would acknowledge my concerns and guide me through my disorders. My name, my address and my phone number are not public. I might be ill, but I am not stupid. When you provide your information to a doctor, and if something weird is going on in your brain, you will get screwed over. The doctor will decide your next step. You will never be able to get the job that you want because your record will tell everyone that you are crazy. Now go ahead, talk to a doctor and ruin your life. Medicine does not care for sick. It cares for the benefit that comes from the sick.

I know I have issues, I have a hard time controlling them, but I have been doing it successfully for years. Right now, I just need to sit and talk to someone who I can trust. I will trust you, only if I know you will not hurt me in any way. If I provide some information to you, you have me in your hand. That is not a nice feeling for a normal person, especially not for an ill one. I will fear you, because what you write about me is a stamp that I must carry all of my life. No, thank you. I do not need a new problem along with an old one. You want to help me? Good, because by helping me you are helping society, the government, finances and at the end, you are helping yourself.

Imagine this! You feel a need to hurt, eat too much, steal something, kill someone, or whichever abnormal need you own; you have someone who will listen to you and help you. The first thing you should do is to go online and search for a "Free Anonymous Psychologist" near your zip code. You will find the address and phone number. Call and make an appointment or in case of an emergency, a "walk-in" is encouraged. Once you are in front of a doctor, introduce yourself anonymously. You can use the name of a fruit, celebrity, a nickname, or whatever you wish; as long as it is

*not your real name. Go ahead and say what bothers you.
The doctor or the therapist will listen and give you some
advice and opinions. In the case if your condition is serious,
the doctor will recommend what the next step is. Even if you
do not follow the doctor's orders immediately, eventually
you will. You will come back, because you will realize that
the doctor is showing you the way to get better. You want to
get rid of your issues; otherwise you would not seek help in
the first place. Just imagine how much better the world
would be if this kind of program existed!*

*At the end, I am an immigrant; an illegal one. Just a
trip to the store is a very dangerous adventure. No wonder
why I have health problems; fear ruins the brain. In this
country, I do not have any rights given to me, so I have to
make my own rights and give them to myself. I have the
right to receive respect, because I gave it to everyone. I
have the right to earn money and give it to my family. I have
the right to be heard and my position to be considered.
Maybe I should have the right to be loved, too, but that is too
much to ask for.*

CHAPTER 8

PAST 2

The taxi dropped her off in Manhattan. Long Island seemed like a faraway country from the safety of Manhattan. She did not leave DevY's house for almost one year, and now she was free; almost free at least. No, she was more imprisoned than ever before, but she did not know it. In DevY's house, she was safe from the immigration service and now, she has the police and immigration after her.

The backpack full of money gave her confidence. Never in her life had she owned that much money. It was time to move on, and also to move into a hotel located in Times Square. In the middle of August she was dressed in black gaudy clothing with gloves on her hands, so she stood out from the rest of the customers at the hotel. The receptionist asked what he can do for her in his professional, but intimidating voice, for he thought that she was wasting his time. As soon as she replied with an accent that she needed to book a room for ten days, he had enough and asked her to leave.

RECEPTIONIST - Miss, I am sorry to inform you, but there is nothing here that will fit your needs.

- Thank you for your advice. Please, may I speak to the manager of the hotel?

RECEPTIONIST - Miss, he is busy dealing with our other clients. He might take a long time to arrive.

- I will wait for his arrival.

The receptionist looked at her, and even though he knew that this woman did not belong there, he was a little afraid that she might actually be somebody important. Successful people are weird, but she was not pretty to him and her accent showed that she was not smart either, so how could she possibly be successful? Regardless, he called his manager. Less than fifteen minutes later, an older gentleman appeared. The receptionist pointed with his head toward the tall woman dressed in black, standing at the side of the receptionist desk with her backpack.

MANAGER - Good evening, Miss. I am the manager. What can I do for you?

- Good evening. You can find a very comfortable room with a Jacuzzi for me, please.

MANAGER - As our receptionist informed you, unfortunately we are booked for tonight. Can I call a taxi for you?

- The place does not seem busy, but I am sure you would not refuse a couple thousand dollars for a profit.

MANAGER - Definitely not, Miss. Let me walk you toward the door.

- You seem like a brilliant man, so please inform me which one is the most expensive hotel in this area.

His sarcastic smile showed that his patience was reaching the limit, but a scene in the lobby would not bring higher ratings to the hotel.

MANAGER - It is the Plaza Hotel, Miss.

- Would you mind to make a reservation for me?

59

He could not hold back his laugh and had to let it out in the most arrogant way. He decided to follow this comedy game and walked behind the desk. One push of a button, and he was connected to the Plaza Hotel.

MANAGER - Miss, how many nights are you looking to stay for?

- I will start with two.

MANAGER - Are you paying with a credit card?

- No, cash.

She opened her backpack and showed the money to the manager. Besides opening the backpack, she also opened her mouth.

- For your information, I can afford to stay in any hotel I want. Even though I do not look rich, I also do not look like someone who writes the most popular blogs online. This hotel will not receive positive feedback, but your boss will receive a note containing the names of the individuals responsible for my experience. Next time, when you and your receptionist decide to reject a customer, turn around your name badges.

MANAGER - Miss, I am sure this was a huge misunderstanding. Let me get you a beautiful room in this place.

- Instead of a taxi, please call a limousine service for me.

MANAGER - Of course, anything for you, Miss.

The manager hung up the phone and fear jumped up to his face. The person on the other side of the line just overheard an interesting conversation.

The limousine dropped her off in front of the Plaza Hotel. She paid up front, even though a very nice receptionist did not request it. He did not want to hear the same words that he heard over the phone a few minutes ago.

She was escorted to her room. She opened her backpack, and then she realized that she made the first mistake of her freedom; two nights in this hotel could buy her a monthly rent in this city. She was hurt and offended by the receptionist's and manager's behavior, so she wanted to make them feel the same way they made her feel. Sometimes, when a teacher teaches other people a lesson, the teacher gets satisfaction, but that contentment is often way too expensive.

***

While living in DevY's house, she did not have Internet access, but she was able to sneak and write short letters to her family; sometimes containing stolen change from DevY, such as twenty or ten dollars. Those letters were placed in the box with DevY's mail and the secretary took care of it once a week. Somehow, DevY never addressed her way of being in touch with her family or maybe he did not know.

In the Plaza Hotel, she did not feel comfortable. The physical pain was unmanageable, but mental fear was able to win over her beaten body and infected fingertips. After a long bath, she managed a few hours of sleep. In the morning, she took a risk, and walked into a Duane Reade drugstore, where she allowed a doctor to check her infected fingers. Even though she managed to get away with a fake name, address and phone number, he did not believe that she accidentally damaged her

61

fingers while handling chemicals in the laboratory. The doctor insisted on the truth, but at the end, he gave up. It was hard for him to believe that a lab technician doesn't have insurance. He prescribed antibiotics for the infection and properly applied dressing on all ten fingers. That was the beginning of putting the pain under control; it was time for her to reorganize her life.

The same morning, she purchased a laptop and a few cheap pieces of clothing. Her old email address was closed due to inactivity. A few minutes later, she had a new email address, and she hoped that her little sister's old email address was still active. Typing with painful fingers, pushed inside big stretchy gloves, was not comfortable.

From: green.card@hotmail.com
To: princessforever@yahoo.com
Subject: Your Sister's New Email Address

My princess, it is your big sister. :) My situation changed and I am in a position where we can email each other as before. Please, write me as soon as possible. I LOVE YOU MORE THAN IT CAN BE EXPRESSED!

She had to find a cheap, secretive residence and some kind of a job that would bring her quick money under-the-table. In reality, she needed a job where she could wear gloves and not look suspicious. A cocktail waitress position was ideal.

In Greenpoint, Brooklyn, a small studio apartment was move-in ready. The same day, she took subway 7 to her potential new place. The studio was a little bigger than a closet, barely fitting a full size bed. The bathroom's stand up shower did not allow her to turn around inside. In the corner of the tiny studio, was a fridge and a stove. Despite it all, what she really loved about the place was the landlord's frustration to finally rent it and no requirements for a social security number or a job letter. She told him that she was a waitress and an artist waiting for her "big break". It seemed he did not care about anything but the money. The same day, he took a copy of her fake driver's license and they signed a lease contract for one year. She paid him a deposit and one month's rent. Her privacy and freedom ended up costing $1,000 a month in this junk place with heat, hot water and electricity included. She moved in the same day. After that long day, she checked her email.

From: princessforever@yahoo.com
To: green.card@hotmail.com
Subject: Thank you God!!!!!!!!!!!!!!!!!

My God, my God, what a miracle!!!!!!! You don't know for how long I was waiting for this day!!!! I love you my sissy, I love you so much!!!! I am so happy that I don't know what to write. Please call us. Write me at what time you want me to be in the neighbor's house. She said you can call us on her phone anytime you want. I was so worried that we will never get in touch again. We received over twenty of your letters and we treat them as a biblical text. Our stepmom said that you are probably in jail, but I did not believe her. I wonder where you have been this entire year. I know you said in letters that you are okay, and that this is your big sacrifice before finally getting your green card, but I want to know why you could not call us or let us write to you. Our little brother is getting even sicker. Being without money was very hard on our stepmom because she could not take him to the doctors. He looks cute, but different than other kids. I think he has many different illnesses. Thank you also for the money, it was a big help. I am still studying English in the local library after my school classes. The teacher told me that I can pay her whenever I get money. I am so glad that I did not lose any time from my education. I know you will take me to America with you and I want to make you proud with my English. Did you get a green card yet? When am I coming to live with you? When I come there, I will work two jobs and you will be resting at home. I will treat you like a queen, because that is what you are. I LOVE YOU MORE!!!! Stepmom is happy that you are back in contact with us. She cares about you, but I think she is the happiest because she has hope again for curing her son. She thinks now you will help us financially again and even bring us all to America. American doctors would cure our little brother in a few weeks. I LOVE YOU!!!! I LOVE YOU!!! I LOVE YOU!!!

The next day, she sent back home $3,000 and it felt so damn good to be useful again. She managed to have a phone conversation with her sister and stepmom. Both of them were thrilled to be able to speak with her. Her little brother was too ill to leave the house, but with new income, he would be able to be hospitalized. Back at home, it did not change a lot in a year. The brother was as sick as before, her stepmom was focused on taking care of her ill son, and her little sister was about to enter middle school. Unfortunately, the green card was still on hold.

CHAPTER 9

January is always the time when New Year's resolutions become broken. She could not afford to break hers. By the end of the spring, she had to close her business and disappear. That was too bad, because business was booming as always. The clients trusted her and the working dolls enjoyed their well-paid jobs. Money was filling up The Doll House owner's account; in this case, EdwarD's account.

DaxoN, the self-proclaimed manager, came into her studio to warn her about a suspicious young man at the bar. This was the boy's second night there, and both nights without a mask. She didn't like at all having someone on her property without having his background checked. She instructed DaxoN to go downstairs and keep an eye on him until she arrived. Quickly, she took off her oversized blue t-shirt and put on brown leggings and a tight brown sweater. Her long, wavy blonde hair was almost reaching the end of her back. The black boots up to her knees kept her feet dry while she was rushing through the snow around the house toward the bar.

At the white bar, there were three masked men lined up. One of them had a Bill Clinton mask. In the left row of the tables, where a big red candle was dimmed, was a boy sitting without a mask. He wasn't moving his eyes from two girls dancing in the middle of the bar. Both girls moved graciously and slowly while "German Dance" by Mozart was playing in the background. She recognized SamanthA. Even though it was dark, SamanthA's sexuality was filling the entire room with tension. The smell of wine mixed with the candles' smoke was making heads spin, but not as much as SamanthA's appearance. That girl knew that she was dancing in a bar where all the clients were gay and maybe a few of them bisexual, but she still delivered a hell of a show. With a big Spanish booty, fake breasts, flat tummy as the result of a liposuction, and dark brown straight hair that reached under her butt, she looked just perfect. Her black sparkly pumps matched with her black glittery underwear. She had a white see-through dress that reached the floor with every movement of hers. She moved slowly and elegantly, while touching every single part of her body. SamanthA was the angel of sexuality.

The boy looked as if he was in his early twenties. In this cold winter, he was wearing a tight black t-shirt and black jeans. His muscles were bigger than Arnold Schwarzenegger's. His skin complexion was nicely tanned and his short black hair perfectly matched his clothes. It would be a big loss for women if he was gay.

She approached him from the side and he didn't even realize that she was standing next to him.

- *Good evening, Mister!*

He just nodded to her in a polite way and placed his sight back on SamanthA.

- *Mister, I am speaking to you.*

He looked at her with confusion and unease. He didn't like this kind of interruption.

- *I am the owner of this place and I would like to talk to you about your visit here.*

Finally, she got his attention, but only for a short time.

ALEX - Hi! I'm AleX. What do we need to talk about?

- This place only accepts customers who book upfront and I do not remember you scheduling this visit.

ALEX - Scheduling a visit to a strip bar? It is not even busy. I don't see any problem with me being here.

- I see a problem.

ALEX – I apologize. I'll schedule it the next time. Excuse me, I would really like to enjoy my glass of wine alone.

She bended down, pulled a gun from her right boot and pushed into his back.

- If you dare to move, security will kill you like a deer.

ALEX - No, Ma'am, I won't move. I think we have misunderstanding.

- Yes, we do and we will fix it. Get up and move toward the door.

He listened to her. Once he stood up, she realized that he was maybe as tall as 6' 2". He was so tall, muscular and yet able to obey. When they came outside, he didn't run away. Instead, he stood under the open sky.

- Are you ready to have a talk with me now?

ALEX - Yes, Ma'am, I am.

- Do not call me "Ma'am". Ma'am is the name for old ladies and even though I am much older than you, I am not allowing you to call me that.

ALEX - I apologize, Miss!

(She smiled.)

- *That is better. How did you find out about this place?*

ALEX - Yesterday I went for a run in these woods as usual, and then I saw a car going through here. I followed the car and ended up at this bar. I enjoyed looking at that girl, so I came back tonight.

She put her gun back in her boot.

- *AleX, are you gay?*

ALEX - No, Miss, I'm not.

- *Good. Would you like to come in my office for a glass of wine?*

ALEX - If you point the gun at me, I will. If I have a choice, I would like to go inside and continue enjoying the show.

- *No, AleX, you will not be forced to have a glass of wine with me. Go inside and enjoy yourself, but before you go in, you have to obey one big rule.*

He was offered two choices of masks. One of them was Dora's face, but he chose the lion's face. AleX, the boy with a body built as an animal's, but weak as a feather, went back in to enjoy SamanthA's perfect looks.

***

Back in her office, she locked the door and felt a new kind of pain: being old and unattractive. She is in her early thirties, but she never imagined that boys in their twenties would look at her as an old lady. Sometimes, she would think that a new kind of pain couldn't reach her, because she already experienced an entire diversity of agony. It was time for Facebook; time to share her uncomfortable realization.

POST "RANDOM THOUGHTS" 62: *What does it mean being old? When are you considered being old? Once you end your twenties, it seems impossible to compete in the men department with women of that age. Tonight, when I saw this young man, I felt an instant attraction to him. I am not sure if "me in my thirties" wants this boy, or the "me in my twenties" is seeking a never-gotten-chance to be with a man of that age group. It was an instant attraction. And even though he rejected me, I still want him. This young kid looked at the glamorous stripper as she was a heavenly creature and I wish I was her.*

Her writing became interrupted with a knocking at the door. She got up from her king size bed and opened the door without caring who was behind it. It was DaxoN.

DAXON - Boss, that boy is still there. He is wearing a mask now.

- I know. I made him put the mask on. He is just some local kid who found this place by luck.

DAXON - He can bring other people here, too.

- I do not think so. He is here because of SamanthA and that is all that he thinks about.

DAXON - He might bring friends to be a show-off. You know how boys of that age are.

69

- No, I do not know, but I know how a man of any age thinks when he likes a woman. She is the only thing that is going through his mind.

DAXON - My man did not come, right?

- You are still hoping that he will come back and that is why you are wearing those sexy jeans with that extra tight shirt? White color suits you well. You have an angelic look just like SamanthA. Too bad none of you will reach heaven to enjoy real angels.

DAXON - I know you want that kid, you cougar bitch. (He laughed.) I will help you have sex with him if you help me have sex again with my man.

- That is impossible.

DAXON - You have his contact information and you can arrange one more meeting.

- No, it is impossible to make that kid like me. He even sees me as an old lady. He even called me "Ma'am".

DAXON - (He laughed again even harder.) Tonight he chose SamanthA over you. Tomorrow he will choose you and then somebody else.

- He did not find me attractive. He did not feel chemistry between us.

DAXON - Only you women care about that chemistry crap. Come on, boss, are you afraid of being a cougar?

- What?

DAXON - SamanthA has age and different looks, but you are forgetting that with age, you get more wisdom and power, so use it. Every age group brings benefits. You have to recognize them and abuse them.

- Keep talking. (She smiled.)

DAXON - If SamanthA is in your way, remove her. That boy is hungry for sex and any kind of new experience. Take a lead. You are the one with the supremacy in this case. Switch the roles.

- Switch the roles? Oh my God, that is what I need. He can be me and I can be EdwarD. This time around, I am above in every way.

DAXON - That is not exactly what I meant, but it seems you are somehow getting my point. Give me five minutes and I will be right back.

He left the studio. It seems that tonight, all men are running around The Doll House in their t-shirts, forgetting that it is January covered with snow. She was sitting at the small coffee table. More than ten minutes later, DaxoN walked back in covered with snowflakes.

DAXON - Your kid left. SamanthA told me that the boy asked her if she would be performing tomorrow night. Because she gave him an affirmative answer, that means that he will be back. Also, he gave her his phone number on a piece of paper, but she lost it. Tomorrow night, I will send him here to you and you can take it from there. In return, the following night, you can bring me my Phantom on the third floor, and I will take it from there. Deal?

- *We have a deal. Go and close the bar, but make sure to send SamanthA upstairs.*

DAXON - Do not kill her. (He laughed.)

- *No, I will just make sure she is not in my way. I am tired of gorgeous women getting everything.*

She was boiling water for a cup of green tea when SamanthA walked inside the studio, wearing a bright red coat which covered half of her red boots.

SAMANTHA - Boss, what can I do for you? Do you mind if I sit on the bed?

- *Go ahead.*

Both women were sitting on top of the bed. Both of them are so different and yet the same.

- *Do you like that boy?*

SAMANTHA - Are you talking about AleX?

- *Yes, I am.*

SAMANTHA - AleX is a young handsome man, but poor, and I don't admire that quality.

- *How do you know he is poor?*

SAMANTHA - His clothes are cheap and he was drinking a cheap wine. I asked him what he does for a living and found out that he is taking care of his blueberry farm.

- *You know he likes you a lot.*

SAMANTHA - Every man likes me a lot, because I use my sex appeal to get where I am heading in life.

- *Where are you heading SamanthA?*

SAMANTHA - I want to be as successful as you are. You don't need anybody and you are making crazy money on your own. You're succeeding without having to use your gorgeous body.

- *What do you mean by gorgeous body?*

SAMANTHA - You're a supermodel. You are so tall and skinny. You look elegant even in those leggings and sweater. Your hair and your legs look like they have no end.

- *This comes from a girl who is able to make gay men question their sexual orientation. SamanthA, you have a huge butt and huge breasts, exactly what men like to touch. Your lips are bigger than your forehead.*

(Both women giggled.)

SAMANTHA - Yeah, collagen injections do miracles. You should get big lips, they boost your confidence; not that you need a boost.

- *You are a sweet girl. What do you do when you are not here?*

SAMANTHA - I am enrolled in SUNY Oneonta, majoring in economics.

- *And you dance here for extra cash?*

SAMANTHA - Yeah…And I have a relationship with a man who has a vacation house in the area and he helps me financially.

- *How old are you for real?*

SAMANTHA - Twenty.

- *You have everything going well for you, and you have plenty of time to make mistakes and fix them. Your beauty will get you far, but right now, I need that beauty far away from here. You are fired.*

Later on that night, she was laying down on her bed thinking about EdwarD and SamanthA. She was wondering if EdwarD would go after SamanthA if he saw her that night when he came to Oneonta. Why couldn't she look like her?

Her mind became overtaken by the thoughts about the little boy in his cold grave. His flesh must be already eaten by warms. Her stepmother is devastated and her little sister faced another loss. Where is the green card? At this point in her life, she was afraid of dreaming about it.

CHAPTER 10

PAST 3

Being a cocktail waitress in a gentleman's club in Manhattan is not considered a decent job. She was showing a lot of her skin, but she couldn't be a stripper. Being a stripper required dance moves, which she could not apprehend. Her strong accent and lean physique set her apart from others in the club. Gentlemen liked looking at her and some of them even offered money to see her on the stage. She wanted money, but if they saw her clumsy movements, they would see her as a clown rather than a sex symbol.

In their early twenties, women tend to think that they have much time in front of them. They are not afraid of acting stupid, because there is plenty of time to correct their mistakes. She was different though, because her destiny forced her to act outside of her age group. The girls at work called her "GlovE", because she was always wearing all kinds of gloves. Soon that became her stage name. Somehow, it seemed that she was living the life of an average American girl. The place in Greenpoint became her cozy zone, where for the first time in her life, she had the privacy and freedom that came with it. Besides that, she also had a fun job where she was meeting men with money and pretty girls who knew how to use their bodies in order to make their livings.

Weeks passed and many new tricks entered her head. Dancing was not a talent; it was the ability to project sexual desire. Her body, apart from her fingers, healed and she became comfortable being different. She did not know at that point, that when you feel sensual, men, like animals, can feel it, too. That autumn night, she put on a red thong, red gloves and a black blazer, while wearing golden high-heel sandals and a sexy golden carnival mask. She did not wear a bra and her medium-size breasts freely moved around while she was proudly walking through the club. Her blonde hair was shaped in long curls. The other girls suddenly could not compare with her. She took all of her imperfections and laid them out, while the other girls presented only their assets. It is well-known that uniqueness brings popularity faster than perfection.

A gentleman in a dark blue suit and glass of expensive wine in his hand, sat at the bar where she was preparing cocktails.

GENTLEMAN - Don't you feel hot in that jacket? I can help you take it off.

- I can help you to fill up another glass of wine.

GENTLEMAN - Both of us are able to do favors for each other, so we can do some kind of business together.

- Are you a police officer?

GENTLMAN - No, sunshine, I'm not, but I can be whatever you want me to be.

- What do you want to be for me?

GENTLEMAN - I want to be the guy sitting in a comfortable chair, looking at you dancing, without that jacket.

- *How bad do you want it?*

GENTLEMAN - Is $1,000 for half an hour bad enough?

- *$2,000 would make you more convincing.*

GENTLEMAN - Let it be.

- *I will meet you in ten minutes in a private room.*

Her boss was surprised that she was willing to start giving private sessions to clients, but there was never objection for extra money. Each girl gave him a $100 for use of the private room.

The dark blue suit looked shiny in a dark room. The red comfortable chair matched his red eyes, which coordinated with her red thong and gloves. The song "Disturbia" by Rihanna was playing in the background. She stood up in front of him, like a statue, looking straight in his eyes for a few seconds. Then she slowly kneeled down in front of him, reached for his hand which she placed on her face, and allowed him to touch her lips with his index finger. Then she placed both of his hands on the collar of her blazer. Slowly, she unbuttoned the only button; her breasts became exposed. She placed his hands on her waist and then her gloves held his hands in a steady position. Her legs were finding their way up between his hands, while their eyes were locked together. Standing above him gave her a chance to look at his crotch, the hard mound pushed against the cloth. She released his arms and slowly started touching her body from her belly button up to her breasts. She circled around her right nipple with her red-gloved index finger, while her left breast was being squeezed by her left arm. Then with both of her hands, she was going through her hair while graciously moving her hips. He placed his hands around her waist and pulled her closer to him. He straightened up his body in the chair and placed his mouth on top of her thong. His tongue was finding a way to her more sensitive area. Even though she was slowly moving, his tongue followed her. His hands were squeezing her buttocks and his tongue was exploring her private area. A heavy breathing was coming out through his nose and mouth. She was looking at the clock on the wall behind his chair.

After half an hour, he handed her money and left the room. It was only $500. She was supposed to ask for the money before the session. Another lesson was learned.

CHAPTER 11

The Jacuzzi was filled with hot water. The entire studio was not only clean, but also disinfected with bleach. Scented candles were spread all over the place. It was time to take care of her body. She shaved her legs, armpits, and private area. She waxed her mustache and plucked her eyebrows. Her entire body was covered with vanilla scent lotion. Her long blond hair was first blow dried, straightened and then curled into big curls. Mascara, eyeliner, and sunny brown eye shadow made her green irises the dominant focus on her face. Light orange lip gloss covered her lips. A plain, long-sleeved, tight black dress above her knees framed her physique. The date was inside the studio, so there was no need for shoes.

Around fifteen minutes to six o'clock that evening, she received a text message from DaxoN, "AleX is coming upstairs. I told him that SamanthA will meet him there. Take it from here."

Knocking at the door made her feel positively nervous. She put the coat on and opened the door. AleX was holding a red rose in his hand and he had a big childish smile on his face. He was wearing blue denim and a dark blue sweater which perfectly fit his muscular body. His black leather jacket was hanging over his shoulder. His big white teeth had the color of snow. Those brown eyes were more kissable than Godiva chocolate. How could such a young boy be so sexy?

ALEX - Oh, hi! I am looking for SamanthA.

- Hi! AleX, right?

ALEX - Yes. The manager, DaxoN, told me to meet
SamanthA in here.

- Come in then. Do not wait outside.

ALEX - Thank you!

*- Please, take off your shoes. I do not like when shoes are
worn in the house.*

He obeyed silently. Quickly, he looked around the place.

ALEX - This is a very interesting and clean place. Did
SamanthA organize this?

*- No, this is my place and it always looks neat. Have a seat
wherever you want.*

He pulled out the chair facing the small kitchen area.

ALEX - Miss, I don't want you to be late wherever you are
going. I can wait by myself.

*- I know you can, but would you leave a stranger alone in
your house?*

ALEX - Most likely not.

*- You know she will not be here until six o'clock. That is the
time when her shift starts.*

ALEX - Oh, I can wait downstairs then.

- No, have a glass of wine with me until she comes.

She took off her long black coat. From the upper kitchen cabinet, she pulled out the bottle of Chateau Ausone, Saint-Emilion Grand Cru, France. She poured the wine into two glasses and placed them and the bottle on the coffee table. He looked at the white label and then took a sip from the glass. She sat at the chair next to him.

ALEX - This sounds and tastes like a very expensive wine. Why are you doing this?

- Because you are my guest and I feel bad for the way I treated you yesterday.

ALEX - I understand that you were protecting your business, Miss. By the way, what is your name?

- Calling me "Miss" does the justice.

ALEX – (He nodded.) What kind of business is this?

- I am not going to tell you my secrets, because then you might become my competition.

ALEX - I doubt it. I am just trying to have small-talk.

- But in reality, you do not care what my answer will be.

ALEX - Miss, I came here to see SamanthA, because I really like that girl. I am not sure what your intentions are, but you seem too pushy and I get uncomfortable. Even right now. There is no need for the two of us to have drinks together.

- You really do not care what comes out from your mouth.

ALEX - From my mouth, comes honesty.

- Good for you. Does it bother you that SamanthA dances almost naked in front of so many men?

ALEX - I feel extremely attracted to SamanthA and I really want to get to know her. I am sure she has reasons why she is doing this kind of work. Whatever she did before, it doesn't bother me at all. But if we start dating, then I will be bothered with wrong things down the road.

- You speak like a man.

ALEX - I am a man.

- While you are in an honest mood, tell me what do you think about me?

ALEX - Miss, you're obviously a successful woman. You're attractive, strong and dominant. Yes, very pushy, but that can serve you if it already hasn't, in your life. Right now, it is after six o'clock and SamanthA is not here. So, you go ahead and honestly, tell me what is going on.

- She does not even know you are here. I set it all up so I can see you. Last time, I asked you for a drink and you rejected me. I did not take that well.

ALEX - You offered me sex from nowhere.

- What is wrong with that?

ALEX - Okay, listen. I'm not attracted to you. I don't like older women, I don't have sex with every woman that approaches me and I already have another woman in mind. On top of all that, you're very weird and I don't like to be part of a game that I didn't agree to play. I am 25 years old, but don't think you can play cougar games with me. (He placed the wine glass back on the table.) Thank you for the wine.

He left the studio in such a rush that he almost slipped going down the stairs. She locked the door and took off her clothes. The rest of the wine in the bottle ended in the sink. The tears from her eyes were pouring out faster than the wine from the bottle.

POST "RANDOM THOUGHTS" 63:

Pain all over again!!!

I feel again the message,
It is my life's repeating passage.
I feel your rejection
So, why the heck is my heart having an objection?
How do I explain?
How do I cover the pain?
Here it comes, the same story again.

When the hope for love is born
So fast everything gets torn,
And every time the same kind of pain is thrown.
Oh, no one knows how much pain I am in,
And always I have been.

This crap has to stop,
My head is jumping on the top.
No more heart, no more,
Now I am with myself in the war!
It is time, finally,
To control myself manually,

Oh, yes I know what is right,
Without my heart, I am very bright!

CHAPTER 12

PAST 4

For an illegal immigrant with a criminal past, there are not so many jobs available. She could work in bars or certain restaurants where sexuality was above criminal record and that was about it. Housekeeper, nanny, elderly caretaker, waitress, secretary and a few other under-the-table jobs required identification and sometimes a criminal record check.

Being a stripper gave her the opportunity to save money and to send back home many presents and envelopes filled with cash. Excitement in the stripping world has a very short life. The girls become old fast, because new faces and bodies are entering on a nightly basis. She was not interesting anymore. So many different adult clubs in NYC, but still the same gentlemen are circling all of them.

Craigslist was still her main source of information. There was an interesting personal assistant position for a busy physician. He stated that immigrants are welcome. What did she have to lose? The doctor needed someone to take care of his office, including cleaning, making coffee, organizing, doing light paperwork, shopping and giving him massages when needed. The girl he wanted was supposed to be fit, pleasant and open-minded.

Her reply to the post was:

"Dear Doctor, it would be my honor to provide assistance for you in your daily obligations. I am tall, skinny, blonde, creative and very open-minded. I am

already looking forward to our professional interview. The main question is if I should wear underwear or not? "

A few hours later, she checked her email and received:

"Underwear is not required for qualifications, but photos are. - Dr. D."

She emailed him a few photos taken by her coworkers in the strip clubs. She was in sexy lingerie in all of them. He replied immediately, "I changed my mind; maybe you should wear lingerie because I would love to take it off. I'll be waiting for you in the Starbucks located on 1585 Broadway. See you tomorrow at 5 pm. Please be entirely dressed in green and I will approach you."

All night long, she was wondering what kind of freak he must be and how different this job would be from stripping. However, at least this time, she was dealing only with one customer instead of many.

In the morning, she purchased green shorts and a green tank top. It was a hot autumn day and there was a big possibility that she would sweat under her arms, so she also purchased a green silk scarf and placed it over her shoulders. Green flip-flops accompanied her summery bright look. Big black sunglasses opposed her long blonde curls. Her long legs had no end even in those flat flip-flops. As always, her long fingers were covered with gloves; this time green.

She sat on the chair with her legs crossed at the table for two. Minutes were passing by and no one was showing up. She said a few prayers in her head, hoping that God might help her change her life through this man. She was checking her emails on her prepaid cellphone when she heard a calm voice saying, "I will definitely make it up to you for waiting. I am DaN. It is a pleasure meeting you." He extended his chubby hand toward her.

This man was not taller than 5' 6". He was dressed in black suit pants and a white dress shirt with short sleeves. His white straight teeth matched well with his genuine smile. Not only was his stomach big, but everything on his body had some extra padding. But still, his voice was suiting, and his confidence was flying around him.

- It is not a big deal. I did not wait too long.

DAN - Wrong answer. A beautiful girl like you should never wait for anybody. Your time is way too precious.

- Thank you, Dr. DaN. Have a seat.

DAN - Let me bring us something to drink. What would you like?

- Just water please.

DaN placed two bottles of water and plain cheesecake in a plastic box on the table.

DAN - I can bet you that this cake is not as sweet as you are, but it will definitely give some taste to your water.

- Thank you. I like sweets, too bad I do not come across them too often.

DAN - That is why they're so precious, because they're meant to be rare in our lives.

He took her hand in his and squeezed it gently.

DAN - Allow me to get to know you. Where are you from?

- I am from a country far away from America in every possible sense.

DAN - Are all of your answers going to be mysterious?

- Not all of them. I just do not like to talk about my past. We are here to discuss the job.

DAN - Very inpatient lady you are. I guess you're more interested to know about me than to talk about yourself.

- Go ahead, Dr. DaN, and impress me.

DAN - I spent fifty years of my life trying to impress myself and I didn't succeed. So, I'm not even going to try to amaze you. Instead I'll inform you about myself. I'm a cardiologist and I truly enjoy my work. When it comes to my clientele, I'm very selective and I don't take everybody. My time is excessively precious to me and I'm not going to teach people who do not want to learn about their health. I am happily married with two extraordinary children. I work hard in every aspect in my life and I deserve to have some fun. That is where you come in the game.

- Why did you want me to wear green?

DAN - I just chose a random color, so I can recognize you among all these people. I figured that not too many people would be completely dressed in green.

- Very original.

DAN - I feel sarcasm in the air.

- And I feel impatience. When do you want me to start? What will be my duties?

DAN - Today is Saturday, so let's start this coming Monday. I'll email you the address. Be in my office at 8 am. You can wear whatever you want, but while working, you will be wearing a lab coat over your clothes. Please don't wear gloves or a lot of accessories. My clients start coming in as early as 9 am, so we'll have enough time for showing around. I have one assistant, LorA, working full-time for me and she can teach you some skills. Basically, in the beginning, you will be her helper. Weekends you will have off. You are allowed for a paid lunch break and your paycheck will be $500 cash weekly. For overtime, you will be paid more plus tips for any extraordinary personal work. Sounds good?

- I have to wear gloves.

DAN - Why?

- Because I burned my fingers and until they heal, I do not want them to be exposed to different bacteria.

DAN - Okay then, wear them. What do you want to be called at work?

- You pick the name. I do not care.

DAN - "MonA". That is name of my first girlfriend.

***

After working three months for Dr. DaN, she
developed many different skills such as taking vital signs,
drawing blood, doing electrocardiograms, BGM's,
medical billing, disinfecting supplies and organizing
clinical and office areas. LorA proved to be a very nice
thirty-year-old girl. Dr. DaN was very patient,
encouraging, calm, optimistic, generous, intelligent, and a
hardworking individual. She felt smart for the first time
in her life. She was working in a strip club once a week
and she was sending that money back home. The private
room never failed to surprise her, but the doctor's office
gave her boredom that she enjoyed.

A few weeks after she started working, she
changed her clothing style. Suddenly, most of her body
was covered and not only because New York was getting
colder, but because she started feeling that she didn't
need to abuse her body in order to survive. DaN became
a blessing in her life.

One December's Friday, Dr. DaN asked her to
work extra hours. When LorA left, he invited her in his
office. He was sitting in his chair with eyes focused on his
computer screen, where he was checking patients' charts.
His office was located on Lexington Ave, so street life was
heard through his office window.

DAN - How do you like your job so far?

- I love it very much and there are no words to describe how much I appreciate your goodness.

DAN - I am glad MonA. How do you feel about me?

- You are extremely good to me.

DAN - You know that a man is never nice to a woman without a reason, right?

- I can always hope for an exception.

DAN - Exceptions in life can exist only temporarily and our temporary finished tonight. Are you in love with me?

- Dr. DaN, I admire you a lot and I thought that our agreement changed. I do not want to ruin our work relationship.

DAN - Honey, there is no work relationship. This was just the part of our agreement. You see, I'm not a good-looking man, but I have money and intelligence. I make women fall in love with my personality, so they don't feel disgusted with my appearance.

- You are being too rough on yourself.

DAN - No, I am being honest with both of us. I am changing your life. You are alone in this country and I am teaching you how to take care of yourself according to moral values. You're a hard-working girl and a quick learner, so it is a pleasure to be around you all day. But, you changed your clothing and forgot that I fell in love

with a girl in lingerie. Not a girl in suit pants and a
blouse that you are wearing today.

- I thought you wanted me to look and behave as a lady.

DAN - If I want sex with a lady, I would do it with my
wife, but my desires are different.

- I understand.

He got up from his chair and walked toward her chair.
He took her by the hand and lowered her on the floor.
He took off all of his clothes while he was standing up,
and his wiggly belly was completely free. His penis was
small and uncircumcised. He pulled her blouse off,
unhooked her bra and pulled her pants off. Then he
ripped her thong. She was lying down on the floor like a
dead body ready to be buried in a grave. He touched her
breast while keeping his eyes closed. When he went for a
kiss, he felt her wet face. He opened his eyes and saw her
face covered with tears.

DAN - You are crying. Why?

- I do not know. I am so sorry.

DAN - Are you enjoying me?

- I, I feel sad.

DAN - Why sad?

- I do not know. Do what you want to do, I am fine.

DAN - When people feel fine, they do not cry.

He put her body in a sitting position and wiped her tears with his fingers.

DAN - May I take off your gloves?

- *Oh, please, please do not. I am begging you, do not.*

DAN - I won't do anything to you that makes you unhappy. I respect women. I didn't expect to see you this way.

- *I am so sorry. You are so good to me and I am making a big deal out of nothing.*

DAN - Do you want to have sex with me?

- *I hate sex.*

DAN - But, you like me.

- *I love you because you are so good to me.*

DAN - Go home, please.

She got up slowly and put her clothes on, besides her ripped thong. Before she left his office, she kissed him on the cheek. He stayed on the floor speechless, confused, and naked. This girl was unique and he didn't know what to do with her.

Monday morning, she came to work and LorA informed her that she was replaced by another girl. The new girl was supposed to arrive for training at the end of the day. As fast as a cheetah, she entered DaN's office.

He was sitting on his chair in his suit. He seemed unsurprised by her loud entrance.

- Why are you doing this to me? Why did you fire me?

DAN - Have a seat, please.

- Please, do not push me out of your life.

DAN - We can't work together anymore. I already found another girl for my arrangement. I'm not going to hurt you again.

- Then do not push me away.

DAN - You know where I am and you can always come to see me. I found another job for you.

- I just want to be around you.

DAN - Sweetie, I don't need you around me. Tomorrow you have a job interview with my wife's friend, KimberlY, who needs a caregiver for her mother. The mother is paralyzed and a little crazy. Anyway, they will pay more than I paid you and there is no sex at all in this job. I think this would be a good fit. KimberlY knows that you are an immigrant and she doesn't mind. I gave you very good recommendations and you will definitely get the job.

- I will miss seeing you every day.

DAN - With time, people forget their feelings.

- Not me.

DAN - Yes, you too, give yourself some time.

- If I sleep with you, will you keep me in your life?

DAN - I don't want to sleep with you anymore. I love sleeping with women who want me.

- I want you.

DAN - No, you don't. You need love, any kind of love, and I need sex. We're on different sides. Good luck on the interview tomorrow. I have a client coming in a few minutes.

- Can I email you?

DAN - Whenever you want. I already emailed you KimberlY's address.

One more person gave her a hope of loving her and then took it away. She loved his compliments, his wise talk and his kindness. She loved the fact of having a normal job and earning money without feeling dirty. This man was nice to her and she ruined it. She had sex with all those nasty men, but she could not do it with a man who was actually nice and respectful to her. It was one more reason for hating herself even more.

CHAPTER 13

February is coming faster than it was supposed to. She took a quick trip to MarrY's house. When MarrY opened the house door, she saw her standing with a big box in her hands.

MARRY - Are you moving in today?

- No, this box is filled with very expensive wine that I might need once I move here.

MARRY - So, you are planning to become an alcoholic. Nice.

MarrY's house was heated with a small fireplace in the family room. Actually one huge open space was invisibly divided into the kitchen, the dining room, and the living room, while the stair case was next to the entrance door. On the second floor, she had two bedrooms and one large bathroom.

The two women were sitting on the floor in front of the fire place while drinking tea and making plans.

- You do not know what it means when you feel the need to punish yourself for letting other people constantly punish you.

MARRY - Oh my dear, why do you feel like that? Why do you hate yourself so much?

- Hating myself feels natural and trying to love myself is new territory; a scary one, too. I hate being scared more than hating myself.

MARRY - But you did so many good things, you are a good person.

- I did more bad things, so bad that only a few people dare to think about them. I heard about the Ten Commandments and after I read them, I realized that I broke them all. God keeps me alive because hell is not bad enough for me.

MARRY - No, my dear, He keeps you alive because you are creating heaven on the Earth for so many people, including me. You gave me strength to continue with my life and you aren't even my daughter. Still, you are doing the duties of my dead children.

- Stop being nice to me, you are making me uncomfortable.

MarrY tried to touch her, but she jumped up and picked up the tea set from the floor and brought it to the kitchen, so she could wash it up. Letting MarrY touch her would mean that she was letting someone comfort her which she considered an undeserved kindness.

She came back and stretched out on the floor.

- MarrY, I am here tonight and I am realizing that I am nowhere. All these years are gone and with them, the time is gone, too. Not only is time as an age gone, but the time as part of life is forever lost. It does not bother me that I already spent more than thirty years of my life. What is killing me, is the fact that I will never be a little girl who enjoys playing Barbie, I will never be a young teenager who

97

is filled with dreams and hopes, and I will never be a young adult who is working toward those dreams. Every year carries a certain purpose and if it is not used at the perfect time, it is lost forever. The only way to lose the opportunity of enjoying the moment is constantly working and living for the future. Fifteen years ago, I lived for my twenties. In my twenties, I lived for my thirties. Now in my thirties, I am living for my forties. This lifestyle is like a loop; once you start it, you cannot stop it until God decides to put an end to the cycle. Then you live forever in the moment, but in a different dimension.

MARRY - And people who live for the moment are constantly being accused of being irresponsible, because they don't think about their future. Either way, people are meant to suffer unless they are able not to care.

- Maybe you are right. I will stop by tomorrow and drop off another box. I do not want DaxoN to become suspicious and he will, if he gets the feeling that I am moving out. Tonight, he will want to see his man.

MARRY - Out of curiosity, how much money did you make in these four years?

- Over four million.

MARRY - Holy Mother, gay sex became more expensive then straight. (She giggled.)

- Rich men go after expensive stuff, so the higher price I put on my male dolls, the more clients I get. The fact that gay sex is still looked down on by society and many successful gay men are already married, my business seems to be a perfect solution to everyone.

98

MARRY - How do you find those good-looking gay workers?

- On Craigslist.

MARRY - And you are not afraid that some of them might report you?

- I am playing with powerful individuals. It is a twenty thousand dollar yearly membership in The Doll House club. Whoever is not wealthy enough will not be able to throw away such money. My workers are always interviewed in public in Manhattan and I always check their criminal record. You know, I have cameras all over the place so I have blackmailing material. At the end, once money and sex start flowing around, everybody is happy.

MARRY - And all that cannot bring you a green card?

- It might, but also it might lower me down. It is too big a risk to take. I might get deported faster than I would be able to blackmail anyone. I just do not feel confident for now to play that game.

MARRY - And all of your money is in EdwarD's name?

- Yes. When he was about to kick me out of his life, he gave me his bank account information, credit and debit cards to use, so I do not contact him if I get into financial difficulties. Also, I was using his social security number to open store credit cards, which at that time, saved me a lot of money when I was sending presents back home.

MARRY - What did he do when he saw money coming into his account?

- Nothing. Every time when I checked the bank account, my money was there. As soon as I started putting money in, he took his money out. Since then, he never took anything, but he also never put any money in. I think he opened a new account.

MARRY - He's waiting for you to fill it up to the roof so he can take everything out.

- No, I do not think so, he does not need it. He is the only son; his parents will leave to him over twenty-million plus the properties.

MARRY - You trust that man too much even though he let you down way too many times. EdwarD is not a good man.

- I am not a good person either and some people still believe me, including you Miss MarrY. I have to go. Give me a good-bye hug and I will see you tomorrow.

MARRY - Darling, drive extra safe in the snow.

CHAPTER 14

PAST 5

She wore black gloves, black suit pants and a long black sweater which reached her knees. Her outfit represented her lack of knowledge in fashion very well. KimberlY's house was located on 78th Street and Madison Ave. Before knocking at the door of the three story house, she said a short prayer in her head. A woman, who was probably the housekeeper, opened the door and guided her to the second floor. There, another woman, who looked like a movie star, approached her and introduced herself as "KimberlY". The housekeeper left the room.

KIMBERLY - Have a seat.

- Thank you, Miss KimberlY.

KIMBERLY - How do you know DaN?

- I used to work for him.

KIMBERLY - Did you sleep with him?

- No, I did not and I have the highest respect for Dr. DaN.

KIMBERLY - MonA isn't your name, right? DaN told me that you're an illegal immigrant. I don't care if you want to tell me your real name or not. I'll call you "SallY".

- Whatever you say, Miss KimberlY.

KIMBERLY - Tomorrow morning, you can go in my mother's apartment and start working. I'm going to email you her address and the job description. Her name is "KellY".

- So, I am hired?

KIMBERLY - Of course, you are. DaN asked me for a favor and my mother is so crazy that only a woman who desperately needs a job can handle her. SallY, the housekeeper, will show you the way out.

KimberlY called all of her staff "SallY".

***

During the winter time, it is very cold in Manhattan. She arrived on 82nd and Fifth Ave, where Miss KellY resided. The Metropolitan Museum of Art was a few feet away.

The apartment was on the fourth floor. At the building's entrance, a doorman opened the door for her and then the front desk receptionist took her information. She was escorted by the doorman to an elevator which brought her up to the Miss KellY's place. There was only one apartment on that floor; she assumed that the other floors were the same. She knocked on the door and then a soft voice told her to come inside. She walked into a huge room which served as a living room, dining room and library. Next to the window, in a wheelchair, was a skinny woman with black hair down to her shoulders.

KELLY - Don't stand there like a fucking statue! Come and shake my hand, paralysis isn't contagious.

- Good morning, I am so sorry Miss KellY. I was just admiring your apartment.

She approached Miss KellY and took her hand with both of hers and shook it. Then she sat on the floor next to her.

KELLY - I guess you don't like any of my chairs. I can feel your freezing hands through those gloves. I hope your heart isn't that cold. What is your name? DonA or SallY?

- I prefer to keep my real name private. You can call me whatever you prefer.

KELLY - And why the fuck can't you say your real name?

- Because, as you know, I do not have legal documents and I prefer not to disclose my identity.

KELLY - Listen, if I want to report you, I can lock you in this place and wait for immigration. Stop being a fucking paranoid freak and tell me your name.

- Miss KellY, my intention is not to disobey you, but please, do not ask me to say my real name.

KELLY - Let me choose a name for you, then. Hold on! Should I call you "Moron, Pig, Poop or Dick"?

- Miss KellY, please understand me. I do not say my real name to anyone, because all my life I was called everything but my name, so my name has lost its value. Even if you

*choose any of the names you just mentioned, none of them
are as bad as the names I used to be called.*

KELLY - You know what? I like you already because
you're crazy. Stand up and look through the window at
the Museum. It's fascinating how many different fucking
kinds of people step on those stairs.

*- It is a beautiful view. With this kind of view, you do not
need a television.*

KELLY - And now, I have you. Now, push me, so I can
show you around. This place has two bedrooms, two and
a half bathrooms and a large kitchen. Get up, PrincesS!

- PrincesS? (She smiled.)

***

Miss KellY was an upscale lady in her late
seventies. Her black hair was nicely put together, no
matter where she was going.   She always wore a suit and
high-heeled shoes. She did her own hair and makeup
while everything else required assistance.

After working at her new job for a full week, she
realized that Miss KellY wasn't as crazy as she expected.
She was not treated as a worker, but as an important
person in Miss KellY's life, who proved to be a great
mentor.

Even though neither KimberlY nor DaN
mentioned that this job was live-in, when Miss KellY
requested from her to completely move into her
apartment, she was surprisingly thrilled with that idea.

Her studio apartment in Greenpoint, Brooklyn became empty and her freedom stayed there, but she did not mind to have a bedroom in a luxurious apartment across from the Museum. Miss KellY hated being lonely and her paralysis prevented her from successfully accomplishing her daily activities. KimberlY visited once in a while and it seemed no one else in the world cared about the old rich lady in the wheelchair.

That day, was the ten day anniversary since she got her new job, and three days since she moved into the new bedroom, which was twice as big as her entire studio in Greenpoint.

That morning, she helped Miss KellY take a bath and wear her black suit pants, golden blouse and her black Valentino "Rockstud" pumps. From there, she left Miss KellY to fix her hair and apply make-up. Her grandson was coming to take her out for a lunch.

While Miss KellY was busy in her bedroom, she decided to find a new book to read among the many books in the open library. Her loose blonde hair was covering her eyes, so she decided to tuck all of it inside her tight black sweater.

EDWARD - Not so long ago, people invented something called the "scrunchie".

She moved her sight from the books on the shelf and landed her prospect on a tall, extremely handsome man. He was wearing navy blue suit pants with a blue dress shirt. In his right hand, he was holding a gigantic bouquet of white roses.

EDWARD - Do you speak English, young lady?

- Yes, I do. Good afternoon, Mister.

She pulled her hair from the sweater and extended her gloved left hand to him. He pulled a rose from the bouquet with his own left hand and placed it into hers. They shook each other's hands while the rose was firmly pressed in between.

EDWARD - Left handshakes are rare. You deserve this rose, not only because you are a gorgeous young lady, but because you are clever, too. Now, my right arm is getting tired. I'm going to the kitchen to put the flowers in a vase and I'll be right back to admire your beauty.

She was standing like a statue with rosy cheeks while examining the rose he gave her; the first flower she ever got in her entire life. This man spoke perfect English and his black eyes were so shiny. Every word that came out of his mouth was accompanied with a small smile. When he came back, she didn't acknowledge his presence for the second time that day.

EDWARD - Did you find anything interesting inside that flower?

- Oh no, I was just taken away by my thoughts.

EDWARD - Your facial expression tells me that those thoughts are pleasant.

- Yes, Mister, they are. I assume you are Miss KellY's grandson.

EDWARD - Yes, I am. My name is EdwarD. It is an honor to meet you.

- Thank you, Mr. EdwarD. I will let your grandma know that you are here.

EDWARD - She'll come out when she's ready. Don't interrupt her beauty routine. What's your name, young lady?

- Your mom calls me "SallY" and your grandma calls me "PrincesS". (She said, embarrassed.)

EDWARD - I didn't ask what people call you; I asked what your name is.

- I cannot say it, I am sorry.

EDWARD - Where are you from, strange young lady?

- Not from the United States.

EDWARD - I see, you want to play games with me.

- No, Mr. EdwarD, that is not my intention.

EDWARD - Too bad, because I was ready to play. Let me know when you are ready for the games.

He moved slowly toward the shelves with books and picked out *Frankenstein*, by Mary Shelley and handed it to her.

EDWARD - Read this one and you will understand better the relationship between my grandmother and my mother. When they argue, grandma calls herself "Frankenstein" and my mom becomes the monster. I think you already know that you joined an interesting family.

- *I am very fortunate to be around your grandma.* (She examined the book in her hand while still holding the rose.)

EDWARD - Do you read a lot?

- *Since I can remember, books were my only escape from reality. Do you like to read?*

EDWARD - KimberlY is my mother, so I had to not only read books with value, but also cheap books so I could learn the difference between good and bad writing. She has a special connection with books and she hoped that I would find it also, but that never happened.

- *Why you do not like reading books?*

EDWARD - I like reading books, I just don't like too much of anything. Read *Frankenstein* and let me know what you think about this piece. There is a lot to learn and I can't wait to hear you speaking about *Frankenstein* with your accent.

- *I hate my accent.*

EDWARD - You shouldn't hate anything about yourself. It would be a sin if you didn't appreciate your attributes and qualities.

Miss KellY entered the living area as if she was in a wheelchair speeding contest.

KELLY - My horrible grandson, come to hug me as hard as you can.

EDWARD - It's not time for you to die grandma, so you'll have to be satisfied with a soft hug. (He embraced her softly like she was made of crystal.)

KELLY - You didn't come to see me for fourteen fucking days.

EDWARD - I apologize, but working as a lawyer doesn't allow me to spend time with my favorite people.

KELLY - Save your shitty talk for your judge. Why did PrincesS get a rose and I didn't?

EDWARD - If you go to the kitchen, you will be pleasantly surprised.

KELLY - Oh, my EdwarD, you'll never lose your charm. Where are you taking your good-looking grandma?

EDWARD - I was planning to take you to a recently opened vegan place downtown. Are you up for a day without meat?

KELLY - I am up for anything with you. PrincesS, are you coming with us?

She looked at her black sweater and jeans, and realized that she could not blend in with those two people in front of her. She knew that it was not polite to eat while wearing gloves, too.

- Thank you so much for the invitation, but I will finish some tasks while you are gone. Have some time alone with your grandson.

EDWARD - Oh, BarbiE, you are so concerned about my grandma. And yes, you look just like a Barbie doll.

KELLY - Yes, she does, only because I'm not able to stand up. Otherwise, we would all know who the woman with the perfect body in this room is.

As soon as Miss KellY and EdwarD left, she ran in her bedroom and started reading *Frankenstein.* When Miss KellY and EdwarD returned in the evening, they found her in the kitchen making a salad.

KELLY - Oh my darling, I've had enough grass for today. Don't make me a salad for dinner, instead order some meat.

EDWARD - I guess you won't become vegan anytime soon.

KELLY - Give me some time. Maybe when I get older, I will. I'm going to call your mother EdwarD, so I can brag to her about my time spent with you. (She wheeled herself out of the kitchen.)

EDWARD - Next time, you should come with us. My grandma was talking about you the whole time. I'm so glad you can handle her.

- As I said before, she is a very pleasant lady. I started reading the book and I am already amazed.

EDWARD - Some books, just like people, are able to astonish you in a few minutes.

- Does that happen to you?

EDWARD - Maybe. (He winked at her.)

She shyly smiled back while cutting cucumbers for the salad. He came around the table and then gently touched her cheeks which became red immediately.

EDWARD - Keep up with the great work, BarbiE. Stay gorgeous until next time.

- Have a great rest of your evening, Mr. EdwarD, and thank you so much for the compliments. I appreciate them.

She admired his confident walk while he was leaving the kitchen. She wanted to follow him to Miss KellY's room so she could spend more time with him, but she could not move. Her emotions were uncontrollable. She placed the salad in the fridge for she lost her appetite. As soon as she heard the outside door close, she started missing him immediately.

That night, when she was helping Miss KellY get ready for bed, her mind was completely occupied by EdwarD. His voice was mature, firm and charming. He gave her the rose and more compliments than she ever received in her life. He respected her and showed a genuine interest in her.

Miss KellY was preoccupied with her own happiness. Obviously, the presence of her grandson brightened her entire day as much as it did for her.

Three days passed since she saw EdwarD and she was expecting his visit every single day. She took her laptop, sat on the chair next to the window facing the Museum, and started typing down her feelings.

How can a man make a woman so happy? Just because of him, I am skipping around all day, listening to happy songs, dancing around, and feeling filled with butterflies. His words are playing over and over in my head like a catchy song. He gave me compliments that make me feel pretty, smart and most of all, alive, in a strange way.

I want to become better because of him, even though I like myself who I am now. His attention gave me a power needed for appreciating myself. If he, who is pure perfection, thinks high of me, how can I put myself low? Oh dear God, thank you for making this man be so kind to me. This feeling I never felt before is so powerful; it gives me even more strength than hate does.

Suddenly everything seems brighter, situations have humor in them, I can smile and smile without a reason. How did I deserve these weird feelings, how do I deal with them? How long will they last? Does this mean that I will act childish from now on? That would be so funny, but it does not really matter, because I like every silly second of it.

With my eyebrows I can reach pretty, funny shaped clouds and my body does not crave for food or water, it is filled with something else. My heart is using a different melody for pumping my beautiful blood. My vision has changed also; I never saw the beauty of the trees in Central Park, architecture of Manhattan buildings, spectrum of cars, or variety of beautiful people on the streets. How is it possible that every person is so beautiful? Oh, how much I love my new sight because it allows me to live in a fairy tale.

And all this I have because of him. When he speaks, I could fly; when he touches me, I could cry happy tears. This feeling is so wonderful that it should be scary if I could care about fear in these moments. Oh God, how could I deserve to feel these unknown emotions? I appreciate so much the opportunity to experience this weird body and soul transformation.

The doorbell woke her up from her daydreaming and she ran to the door to pick up the food. She chatted with the delivery guy for a while because he was complaining about the cheap bastards that lived in the same building. They always tipped him only two dollars each time. When she came back to the living room, she found Miss KellY reading her personal thoughts written on the laptop.

- Miss KellY, what are you doing? (Her voice shook.)

KELLY - EdwarD speaks with everybody the same way. Everyone becomes obsessed with him and he knows it. He didn't feel anything special for you, I assure you.

- Miss KellY, those are my private thoughts.

KELLY - What are you thinking, you stupid woman?

113

He is almost forty years old and you are in your early twenties. He could practically be your father.

- Please, can we speak about something else?

KELLY - Leave the food in the kitchen and come in my room to speak to me about EdwarD, that asshole. Hurry up.

She walked slowly into Miss KellY's room, feeling that she was in deep trouble.

KELLY - Sit on my bed and listen very well to what I have to tell you.

She sat at the edge of the bed and looked at Miss KellY's eyes to see if there were signs of disappointment.

KELLY - You're young and just because of your age, you can afford to act stupid, but he doesn't have an excuse for flirting with you.

- He did not flirt with me. He was just being nice.

KELLY - I know him very well. He was fucking flirting with you. You saw a good-looking successful man giving you compliments, and you're immediately giving your fucking heart away? What are you thinking?

- I can control myself.

KELLY - No woman can control her emotions. We're created to be stupid around men we like. Don't forget, I've spent more than seventy years in this fucking world.

- I appreciate your concern.

KELLY - I'm not concerned about you or him, I'm worried about myself. I can't live alone and because of him, you'd leave me.

- No Miss KellY, that will not happen. I misinterpreted his behavior and I just got carried away with everything about him.

KELLY - Keep in mind that if he is really as great as you think, some woman in this world would have grabbed him by now.

CHAPTER 15

February approached The Doll House and she became more anxious than before. DaxoN stopped insisting on an arranged date with the politician. It is always the silent people who are the most dangerous ones.

That night, she decided to pack all of her important stuff up and move in with MarrY; a twist in her love life occurred. While she was mentally saying goodbye to her studio apartment, a knock at the door brought her back to reality. She opened the door and there was EdwarD, wearing his job attire: a suit, a tie and fancy shoes.

EDWARD - Well, well, BarbiE, you are ignoring my email with such ease.

- Hey, handsome, come in. I did not get a chance to check my email. I called my family so I knew they would not email me.

EDWARD - Are you okay? You don't seem your usual self.

- Why? What is different?

EDWARD - There's no excitement and I'm right in front of you.

- Can we meet some other time and I will explain to you some stuff?

EdwarD closed the door and walked toward the bed. He examined the clothes in the suitcase.

EDWARD - Are you going on vacation without me?

- *EdwarD, I am running away from everything. Do you want to come with me? Please, come. Help me get my green card. We can find a solution together.*

EDWARD - BarbiE, I have a family. I'm a married man and I'm not going to abandon my wife. You know that I'll always help you with everything as long as I don't have to change my life.

- *You do not understand. I am under so much pressure. Time is flying way too fast and I have to make smart moves quickly.*

EDWARD - Wherever you go, keep in touch with me and if there's anything I can do, just let me know.

- *Are you listening? I am asking you to come with me. I love you, damn it! We have a past and you know you love me back. For once in your life, put my feelings before yours.*

EDWARD - I'm a married man. MelanY is not going to pay for my mistakes.

- *So, why the heck are you here? Go and be with her, I did not call you to come.*

EDWARD - Stop being a bitch and try to understand me! I have my mother, my father and my wife on one side and you and your family on the other. I love all of you, but in different ways. It's like choosing which arm to give up. How do I run away with you and hurt my family? How do I let you leave and give up the most amazing moments of my happiness? When I'm next to you, I feel happy... and I don't feel that way around anyone else.

A hard and fast knocking at the door disturbed their conversation.

- Who is it?

ALEX - It is me, AleX. Please, open the door. I have to speak to you.

She looked at EdwarD and suddenly, pushed herself off of the mattress, grabbed the Dora mask from underneath the bed, and gave it to him.

- For your privacy, please put this on and leave here. I do not want AleX to see you. Wait for me in the bar and I will meet you there.

EDWARD - Is he your boyfriend?

- No, he is not!

EDWARD - BarbiE, I wish you luck whatever you decide to do.

He put the mask on his face and walked toward the door. He opened it and faced AleX who was rushing inside to pass him.

ALEX - Was that Dora guy your boyfriend?

- No, that was not my boyfriend. What do you want AleX?

ALEX - I need your help. I can't hold my feelings anymore. It sounds weird, but not knowing the truth is killing me.

- *Yes, tell me what you feel. And that guy is just one of the customers. He is gay; otherwise he would not put on that Dora mask.* (She giggled.)

ALEX - That's not my concern. I just didn't want to interfere into your private life. I'm here to beg you to give me SamanthA's phone number so I could reach her. I don't know if you know the feeling of wanting someone so bad, that you would dare to do crazy things just to find out if you have a chance of taking it to a higher level.

- *Unfortunately, I do know.* (After she exhaled a deep breath, she took a piece of paper from the kitchen drawer and wrote SamanthA's cellphone number and handed it to him.) *Go and give your love to the stripper who is dating a married man. She and I are the same kind of garbage, but obviously we have different luck. Go and be with the woman who called you "cheap and poor". With that kind of a stupid brain, you deserve to be abused by her.*

AleX was confused and in shock. She opened the door and with her hand, showed him to get the hell out of there.

She took her purse, suitcase and backpack, stopped at the bar and found the Dora mask on it. EdwarD was nowhere to be found. When she was passing by her mailbox, she grabbed all of her mail. She placed her belongings in the trunk and took the mail with her to her car. There was a utility bill, some junk mail and an envelope without a sender's address. She opened and read a thank you card: "I truly appreciate your loyalty and concern for my family. Thank you for keeping my secret safe and having my back. If you ever get the chance, please let DaxoN know that I truly love him, but I have to choose my wife, my son and my status over him. I hope one day he will forgive me. Your email opened my eyes. Thank you for watching out for the interest of my family as always. - The Phantom of the Opera"

She placed the card back in the envelope. Then she crossed her name on the front side and wrote DaxoN's name and left it back in the mailbox.

She looked back at the empty Doll House. Everything was going according to plan. DaxoN was supposed to come to work at 6 pm and when he comes, he will not find her there. The rest of the dolls and all the clients received an email that The Doll House was being shut down.

The most shocking event of that evening was the fact that she chose AleX over EdwarD, and she could not understand why the hell she cared so much about that kid. She couldn't even imagine how much happiness and pain that boy would bring into her life. Even after her death, he would make sure that the memory of her stays alive.

CHAPTER 16

PAST 6

While Miss KellY was shopping online for her new suits and shoes, PrincesS was preparing breakfast. Each time when she handled food, she wore latex-free gloves over her colorful ones. She prepared for herself two slices of whole wheat bread, a cup of green olives, half of an avocado sprinkled with sea salt and a glass of mineral water. She wanted to finish her meal before Miss KellY would come in because she tried to avoid preaching about the benefits of meat. For Miss KellY, she prepared two hard-boiled eggs, four strips of turkey bacon, two balls of mozzarella cheese and a glass of milk. One woman avoided meat and the other one carbohydrates.

The phone rang while she was eating and that meant less of a chance of avoiding Miss KellY's preaching about the benefits of eating meat; especially, if the caller was KimberlY, who always asked a million questions.

- Good morning, Miss KellY's residence.

EDWARD - Good morning, BarbiE. I couldn't ask for a better beginning of a day than to hear your voice.

- Mr. EdwarD! Thank you. When are you coming?

EDWARD - Why should I come? I'm sure no one misses me over there.

- Miss KellY constantly speaks about you.

EDWARD - I apologize. It must be very boring listening about me, then you're forced to think about me.

- Very funny. You have nothing to worry about; I learned not to absorb the conversations which include your name.

EDWARD - I guess I have to change my name and find one that will enable thoughts about me to enter into your mind.

- The rose did you justice. It is still alive and reminds me constantly of you.

EDWARD - I'll make sure to bring more of them so you can spread them all over the house.

- So, when are you coming?

EDWARD - Let me ask my grandma that question.

- Mr. Edward, before I hand the phone to Miss KellY, I just want to let you know that I finished the book. I cannot wait to see you and talk about it.

EDWARD - I'm afraid I won't be able to visit you guys anytime soon, but you can email me your opinion before any smart idea escapes your intelligent brain. Do you have a pen?

She unclipped the marker from the board on the wall next to the fridge and quickly erased the shopping list with her hand.

- I am ready.

EDWARD - edward.NYC@gmail.com (He spelled it for her.)

- Thank you so much. I will email you tonight. Have an amazing day filled with happiness and success!

EDWARD - Thanks gorgeous, you, too.

She put him on hold, ran to Miss KellY's room and passed her the phone. This kind of conversation was always allowed to interrupt her meal.

***

That night, she placed the rose next to her on the bed, so she could become even more inspired while writing her impression of *Frankenstein*.

From: green.card@hotmail.com
To: edward.NYC@gmail.com
Subject: My Impression of Frankenstein

Dear Mr. EdwarD,

Thank you for being so kind to me and finding time to hear me out. I am so mad at Frankenstein that I decided to write him a letter. Yes, I might be a crazy woman. ;) Please, do not judge my English. In case you did not realize: I am not American. ;)

Here it goes…

Frankenstein, by Mary Shelley

To Frankenstein

My gratitude for an opportunity to write you a letter cannot be fully expressed, but my opinions can be written with ease. Before I continue, I would like to introduce myself. I am a modern Walton; someone who knows your story and also the wretch's. This is my opportunity to stand up for another creature who never knew the feeling of having someone fight for him. Please, read my words carefully and try to understand my frustration. You and I can teach people to see each other, not only with their eyes, but with their soul. Happiness is something that everyone wants. However, not everyone can achieve it; and many who are happy, do not recognize it.

Victor, you were the first born child of a wealthy family. Your ancestors had been, for many years, very important political figures in Genevese, your home republic. At birth, you received unconditional love from your parents. Since childhood, you were exposed to an education without any limits. You were curious, eager to learn, and dedicated to your goals. Family, friends, and professors were your support on a daily basis. A wonderful woman has been chosen to be your bride and traveling around the world has been your reality. It seemed that you were the happiest person in Genovese. You wanted more; without knowing it, you wanted to be God. After much hard work, you achieved your ultimate goal; you created a creature, just like God created a human. That was the point when your life entered the world of misery.

The wretch, the imperfect human, was created by you, man. He did not have ancestors, wealth, opportunity for education, nor women waiting for him; he only had himself. His creator, you, abandoned him. The wretch had a passion for learning, will for helping others, and he was dreaming about happiness, too. His dream was to be accepted; to fit in this world. Even though he worked very hard, he never achieved his goal.

To begin with, I believe that you, Victor, never realized how much responsibility your ultimate goal required. For many years, you have been planning how to make a creature, but you did not spend any time thinking about what to do with the creature after it is made. It turned out that the wretch was not what you expected him to be, and instead of trying to figure out how to fix its problems, you ran away. Your responsibility was to take care of him because you wanted him in this world. You were his parent. The wretch tried very hard to build his life on his own, but he failed, and he came back to seek help from you.

Why did you reject him? Why did he look disgusting to you? You were the one who chose each part of his body and you connected all of them so you were supposed to know how he was going to look. Why were you so surprised by something that you looked upon for so many years? You touched, with your hands, each tissue, and later on, you could not just look at him? You judged him by his appearance and you are the one who made it. He wanted help from you, he did not enjoy doing bad things; it was his way of getting attention from you. You only listened to him, because you were afraid of him; you did not want to lose any other member of your family. If you did not believe that he killed your little brother, you would never take time to listen to his story. The first time

125

you finally listened what he had to say, was because you wanted to know what happened to your brother.

You never cared what he was going through and he knew that. "Believe me Frankenstein: I was benevolent; my soul glowed with love and humanity: but am I not alone, miserably alone? You, my creator, abhor me; what hope can I gather from your fellow-creatures, who owe me nothing (p.66, Shelley)?" The wretch only wanted acceptance from you. He needed you in his life because you were the one who owed that much to him. His attention was never to hurt someone, but after others hurt him so many times, he just wanted revenge. He blamed you for everything. He never planned to kill anyone, especially not a child. When he saw the little boy, he was hoping to be accepted. He wanted to raise a child who would become his companion. However, his plan was crushed before it started.

When he got hurt, the pain and the anger took over his body and mind; and he ended the child's life. "Suddenly, as I gazed on him, an idea seized me, that this little creature was unprejudiced, and had lived too short a time to have imbibed a horror of deformity. If, therefore, I could seize him and educate him as my companion and friend, I should not be so desolate in this peopled earth (p.96, Shelley)." After he accidentally ended the child's life, he discovered a new feeling called "revenge". He says, "I, too can create desolation; my enemy is not impregnable; this death will carry despair to him, and a thousand other miseries shall torment and destroy him (p.97, Shelley)." The wretch acted like many human beings would; he was hurt, so he wanted to make the person responsible for his suffering, pay for what he had done.

When he realized that he would never get anything from his creator, he asked for someone like him, because he already tried to make a connection with other humans and he did not succeed. Frankenstein, I am truly impressed with your selflessness. You sacrificed your own family for the benefit of the world. You could have saved yourself from the pain, but the price would be paid by possibly, all human kind. The wretch had the capability to do many evil things and with time, he would have learned exactly how far he was able to go. You made the right decision for not creating another imperfect human, but you were wrong for not taking care of the one that already existed. You could have been his friend. He needed attention and just a little bit of love. Victor, you were supposed to help him fit in this world.

Instead, the creature was left to feel this way, "I am malicious, because I am miserable; am I not shunned and hated by all mankind? You, my creator, would tear me to pieces, and triumph; remember that, and tell me why I should pity man more than he pities me? Shall I respect man, when he contemns me (p.98, Shelley)?" The wretch suffered so much and it was not his fault that people hated him. He tried to deserve kindness from people.

The De Lacy family benefited a lot from him. Every morning, they had piles of wood left behind their house by some wonderful creature. The old man actually liked him but as soon as he felt his hand, he realized that it did not feel like normal flesh did, so he immediately felt rejection toward him. I wonder how much happiness the De Lacy family would gain if they had accepted him; with his strength and will to work, he could have done so many chores for them. The De Lacy family did not give time or an opportunity to get to know the creature; their judgment was based on what they saw with their eyes.

You had happiness, but you did not appreciate it; you wanted more. You had health, a wonderful family, wealth and a loving fiancé, but it wasn't enough for you. On the other hand, the wretch desired to have only one piece of what you possessed, and that would have been happiness for him. Unfortunately, the wretch never got anything that you treasured.

You, Victor Frankenstein, and the wretch still exist and always will. One day I am you; I do not appreciate what I have and I desire for more without thinking about the consequences. Other days, I am just a wretch who does not fit in this world and who is constantly judged by others. There are so many people who feel this way. It is time to change myself and teach others what the right thing is to do. Frankenstein, I learned from you that I should give a chance to people to show who they truly are. Right now, my eyes do not see what is on the outside, but they focus more on what is inside each person.

BarbiE

P.S. Mr. EdwarD, somehow I do not know where to place you in my life and how to look at you. In my eyes, you are perfect outside and inside.

CHAPTER 17

Waking up in MarrY's house was a pleasure. It was such a quiet place where she and even her mind could relax. During breakfast, she told MarrY the entire story about AleX and how much she was attracted to him.

MARRY - Maybe it is a good idea for you to get involved with someone right now. You'll go crazy hiding in these woods. This isn't your lifestyle. It's too slow for your taste.

- Too slow? I need calmness. But, it would be nice to have AleX, too.

MARRY - Go visit him.

- I do not know where he lives.

MARRY - Use your brain! He said he was going running when he found your house of sin. That means he lives near your business. You got information from DaxoN that he owns a blueberry farm. How many of them are in the area?

- You are right. I should go on a run and enter his property.

MARRY - Go ahead girl and get what you want. Don't go with your car. If DaxoN reported you, I'm sure he'll tell them about your car. You have all day long in front of yourself. Take my car until you get close and then jog toward your old business. On the way there, ask people about the blueberry farm.

Before noon, she left MarrY's property and drove around the area. She stopped by a local supermarket, asked the cashier about the farm, and received simple directions. It turned out that there were only two blueberries farms in the area.

She drove to the first farm and was surprised to find a large house at the entrance. She parked MarrY's car in front of it. Before she left the car, she checked her hair and make-up in the mirror. Suddenly, she realized that she had no excuse to be here. It was still cold and the summer seemed far away. She couldn't use the excuse that she was looking to buy blueberries. When she looked outside, she saw an old man leaving the house. What the heck? She will have to use the oldest excuse ever.

- *Sir, excuse me! Hi!* (She approached the old man who seemed undisturbed by her presence.)

MARVIN - What can I do for you?

- *I am lost and I need the directions to the center of Oneonta.*

MARVIN - I thought you stopped by to get some fresh milk.

- *Oh that would be great. Either way, I was planning to go to the store and by some.*

MARVIN - My name is "Old MarviN" and I supply the entire neighborhood and their neighborhoods with dairy goods.

- *It is a pleasure to meet you. So you own this farm?*

MARVIN - I have help, but it is in my name. Do you want to get a tour of my farm? You'll get to meet all six cows.

*- Maybe some other time. I just moved in the area and I
would like to explore around. Let me just get the milk today.*

MARVIN - Welcome, kiddo! Go do your exploring and my
grandson will drop you off the milk.

- Grandson?!

MARVIN - Yes, he is taking care of the blueberry farm, so
in the summer, you can bake cakes and make fresh juices.

*- You know what? I will go to Oneonta some other time,
now I can explore your farm.*

MARVIN - Good choice. Follow me!

He took her to the stables where she saw the
machines for milking and she got a tour of the food supply
room. The best part was when they reached the open
meadow where six cows were enjoying their cool afternoon
while snacking on the grass.

- It is beautiful out here. So peaceful...

MARVIN - New York saved the best for upstate.

- May I pet a cow?

MARVIN - Kiddo, you know they smell, but go ahead.

She approached a black and white cow who didn't
object being patted on the head. For more than ten years,
she never felt so close to her home than today. This cow
filled her heart with warm feelings. She felt homesick more
than ever before.

They went back to the house where he gave her two plastic containers filled with milk as a welcoming present.

- Thank you so much for the tour and the milk.

MARVIN - You are welcome and come back soon.

- I definitely will. Hold on for a second, please. (She walked to the car and took a piece of paper and a pen from her purse. She wrote her new address on it.)

- Here is my address. (She handed it to MarviN.) *Please, ask your grandson to bring me two more containers of fresh milk tomorrow morning.*

MARVIN - What are you going to do will all that milk? Are you going to make cheese?

- Yes, I will. I did not make it in years, but I am sure I will remember how. Bye, Mr. MarviN.

- Just "MarviN" is fine. Even "Old MarviN" is fine.

- It was a pleasure, MarviN.

***

She arrived home excited. MarrY was busy cleaning the kitchen. She placed the milk in the fridge and some groceries from the supermarket.

- MarrY, tomorrow we will make cheese.

MARRY - I don't know how to make cheese.

- I will teach you. AleX will deliver more milk tomorrow morning.

MARRY - What? AleX is selling blueberry milk?

- Haha. His grandpa has his dairy farm next to AleX's farm.

MARRY - Oh my goodness. You met Old MarvIN.

- Yes! You could not tell me about that farm?

MARRY - That place is not really close to your brothel. How many miles did AleX run that evening? This farm is closer to East Meredith than to Oneonta.

- I guess we are talking about the same people.

MARRY - A couple of years ago, when my family was alive, we used to buy dairy products from them all the time. His grandson was a kid then.

- He still is a kid.

MARRY - You know what I mean. Is MarviN's daughter still there?

- I do not know. I cannot believe you know AleX.

MARRY - Honey, this is not New York where everyone knows everyone, this is upstate where everyone touched everyone.

CHAPTER 18

PAST 7

Most mornings, she wakes up around seven o'clock so she can start her chores before Miss KellY wakes up. She was wearing a white night gown, a purple robe and purple gloves. While she was ironing Miss KellY's sheets, the reception desk called to inform her that Mr. EdwarD was on his way up. She rushed out of the laundry room, which was a hidden part of the large kitchen, toward her bedroom to change her clothes, but it was too late. When she entered the kitchen, EdwarD was entering with the box in his hands.

EDWARD - I have something for you. Look! (He placed a tall white box on the kitchen counter.)

She touched the box with her purple gloves and the smile on her face was shaking from excitement.

- Why did you do this for me?

EDWARD - You deserve my kindness because you're a terrific young lady. Open it already! I'm becoming inpatient.

She took the knife and cut the box open. It was a "Barbie doll" cake! The Barbie, made out of sugar, was standing on the table. She had a long, puffy dress covered with pink icing and decorated with strawberries. A real Barbie doll from the waist up was sticking out of the cake dress. The top part of dress was made out of whipped cream. The Barbie's hair was pulled back in a ponytail and a tiny pink rose, made out of sugar, was embedded in it.

- Mr. EdwarD, I have no idea how to thank you! This is too beautiful.

EDWARD - That is what you look like, except you're a little sweeter.

She looked at him with her happy eyes and wondered if she should hug him. Emotionally, he seemed out of her reach, so she decided to hold back.

EDWARD - BarbiE, now you're not alone. You have someone just like you in front of your eyes. She is beautiful, sweet and unique. In your paper about *Frankenstein,* you indirectly implied that you feel empty and lonely.

- So, you did read my email.

EDWARD - Not only read, I understood it. I wish I was able to make this cake, but even my expertise has limits.

- You have no limits. You are the most amazing man I ever came across in my life.

EDWARD - It's always nice to chat with a young woman like yourself, because your lack of experience doesn't allow you to see things the way they are.

- I see more than I should. And what I do not see, I feel.

EDWARD - Beautiful, take the Bible and read it as a classic literature text. It might fill up the emptiness inside you.

He bent down and kissed the Barbie doll.

EDWARD - I have to kiss one more lady… (He paused) I'll go to wake up my grandma.

Before he left the kitchen he gave her a big childish smile.

- Mr. EdwarD, thank you a million times for everything.

She rushed in her room and put on some jeans and a white t-shirt. Quickly, in the bathroom, she applied mascara and lip gloss. She left on the same gloves and rushed out of her room. When she was passing by the library, she stopped and looked for the Bible. It took her a while to find it. She wondered how long EdwarD would stay with his grandma. She decided to take a glass of water and vitamins to Miss KellY's room as an excuse to see him.

As soon as she opened the kitchen door, she wanted to scream. Miss KellY was sitting in her wheelchair, while wearing only her nightgown and slippers, and she was eating the cake. Almost the entire side of the Barbie's cake dress was gone.

- Miss KellY, what are you doing???

KELLY - Eating breakfast.

- This cake is something special and it is not your breakfast! How did you even get into the wheelchair?

KELLY - My grandson helped me before he left. And hell yeah, this cake is special! It tastes delicious.

- You should have not eaten my Barbie cake.

KELLY - What is wrong with you people? You don't want me to eat meat and now you don't want me to eat sugar? What the fuck do you want me to eat? Did KimberlY ask you to starve me?

- Miss KellY, EdwarD bought this cake for me and it is very important. I did not even get a chance to admire it before you killed it.

KELLY - Oh, that would be such a horrible thing for me to do if I cared. What? You wouldn't let me have a slice? What would you do with it? Bring it to your room and cherish it?

- Not anymore. What a morning this is!

She took a fork and joined Miss KellY in the process of eating the rest of the dress.

- Let's go prepare you for the day. Today you have a doctor's appointment. I guess we do not have to worry about breakfast.

***

KimberlY came over and took Miss KellY to the doctor's office.

She finished ironing, vacuumed the entire apartment and straightened up Miss KellY's bedroom.

She called home to make sure that her family received the packages. Their neighbor was thrilled that their house was used as a local post office. She paid them for using their phone.

Also, since she started working for Miss KellY, she became an online shopper, so she was spending a lot of time buying clothes, shoes, school supplies and even cosmetics for those overseas. Her stepmother, sister and the little brother became famous, because their family member was sending goods to almost everyone in the village.

This late afternoon, she had some time left for herself. The half of the Barbie's body was washed and placed next to the dry white rose on her night table. Now, the Barbie looked exactly like her: half of her still existed and the other half was destroyed. She took the sugar rose from the Barbie's hair and ate it. Then she placed a kiss on the Barbie's head, the same spot where EdwarD's lips were not too long ago. The Bible on the bed grabbed her attention. She did not read it for years and now she decided just to skip through the pages because EdwarD asked her to do so.

From nowhere, thoughts about DaN came to her mind. Since the last time she saw him in the office, she only emailed him once to thank him for her new job. He never replied back. She missed him and time did not change her feelings for him. She was thankful for meeting EdwarD, because he was a great distraction from everything.

The Bible pages with oracles reached straight into her heart. She knew very well that oracles are speeches given by men who claimed that they were delivering God's direct messages. She wished to write one herself and place it straight into the Bible. That was impossible, but placing her own oracle in an email was conceivable.

From: green.card@hotmail.com
To: edward.NYC@gmail.com
Subject: The Oracle

Dear Mr. EdwarD,

    I am reading the Bible as you told me to. I am going to share some more of my thoughts with you…

    Also, thank you for the rose, compliments, cake and every kind word. I do not know how to pay you back for all of your generosity. I do not understand why you are so great to me.

    I hope to see you soon and spend some more time with you. Your presence makes me so happy. You are an amazing person.

    By the way, thank you for reading my emails!

Here is my oracle… ;)

Judgment Oracle

The American nation, all the way from the border of Mexico, from the South of America,
to the North, up to Canada, including Hawaii and Alaska.

You have forgotten your origins and you are against your own people,
which are my people, too.
You offered immigrants to serve you and to do jobs that you do not desire,
and never looked at them as your equal.

139

You never gave the same opportunities to their children,
immigrants' children born on this land,
as to your children and children of your fellow Americans'
children.
You are expressing anger toward the immigrants,
but not toward your own ascendants,
your own blood,
who came to this country for the same reasons as today's
immigrants.

Therefore, you shall taste their destiny made by you, on
your own skin
and the skins of your children.
America shall be destroyed by recession,
Europe shall gain the highest prosperity yet.
You and your children shall leave your house,
graves of your loved ones,
and the land that became yours at your birth,
and move in a new world called Europe,
where you and your children shall be the immigrants,
reliving the same destiny as the immigrants in America.

The children of your children shall free themselves from
the curse,
by realizing how prejudiced their fathers and fathers of
their fathers
were to their immigrant brothers and sisters and their
children.
Those children shall return to the land of America
with their fellow European brothers and sisters.
They, altogether, shall make America a prosperous land
once again,
the land where every immigrant who follows God's word,

shall belong to the land as much as any other of God's children.

The land of America shall become filled with my chosen people
who shall make peace in the entire world
and who shall spread the word of God
from the deepest parts of the ocean to the highest clouds in the sky.

Mr. EdwarD,

This oracle paints the image of God as a fair father who treats all of his children with the same firm hand and a loving heart. Once the children stop behaving in the proper way, it is time for a time-out, so they can learn from their mistakes and not repeat them.

BarbiE

CHAPTER 19

MarrY entered her kitchen to find out why there was so much noise.

MARRY - Good morning, Miss Pathetic!

- What is wrong with you, MarrY?

MARRY - Sweetheart, it is seven in the morning and you're wearing a sweater dress and high heel boots. Where do you think you are?

- Do you know who is coming here this morning?

MARRY - Why do you think I called you pathetic?

- Come on MarrY, show some support. I already made for us some tea and pancakes. If you are nice to me, I will let you eat some of the cheese that I will make today.

MARRY - You made a lot of noise, too. Leave those pots alone and sit down. (She took a bite of a pancake and a sip of tea.)

- I have to listen to you. I am living under your roof. (She smiled.)

MARRY - What is going on?

- I am making you breakfast and I am excited to see sexy AleX.

MARRY - Why?

- Because you are hungry. (MarrY gave her a serious look.)
Okay MarrY, I do not know why I am doing certain things.
Do I look ugly in this dress? I guess blue is not my color.

MARRY - I was thinking something. You know, you'll never get papers and you are already wealthy. Why don't you take your money and return home to be with your family?

- I lived with you less than three days and you already want me out?

MARRY - Please, be serious.

- A million times, I wanted to go back. As soon as I killed DevY, I knew that I had a tiny chance of getting a green card. I stayed to make money, and then I wanted to find a way to bring my family, so my brother could get cured here. Now, I do not have an excuse for being here, but I still am.

MARRY - What is the real reason that you stayed? I mean, you have all this money and you could have an amazing life there.

- I cannot enter into my country. I could go somewhere else and start my life over, but I have no identity. Legally-looking, I do not exist.

MARRY - Why can't you go back?

- You already know too much about me. (She took a deep breath.)

MARRY - If you talk to someone, you could clear your mind.

143

- I do not have a mind to clear. Here you are, here is your answer: I killed someone there, too… DevY is not the first person I ever killed.

MARRY - Who?

- Do not ask me again. I am not going to tell you, because I am not going to relieve my past by talking about it.

MARRY - However you want my dear. I respect your silence. I am sure you have had a great reason for that.

- What time does milk usually get delivered?

MARRY - (She smiled.) I never had it delivered before.

- Do you think I look ridiculous?

MARRY - Why do you want that kid?

- Because I never had a man that I wanted. This time, I will not quit until I make sure he wants me.

MARRY - Didn't EdwarD want you?

- Oh please, MarrY, I am not dumb anymore. I know he does not want me as a woman. As a whore, yes.

MARRY - Just out of curiosity, I have to ask you this. How come you don't mind being with a married man?

- I touched many married men.

MARRY - Why?

- I have my reasons.

MARRY - More silence from your side?

- Yes.

MARRY - I wish to know what is going inside your mind so I could help you.

- It is empty, MarrY. I feel things and then I block them. I became cold. I do not over-think my actions. I am driven by an impulse.

MARRY - How do you feel right now?

- Nervous on the surface. I do not know how AleX will react when he sees me. If I look deeper inside myself, I feel painful love for EdwarD. Then I go deeper and I find myself feeling guilty for my brother's death. I feel guilty for my sister being raised by a woman who is not her blood. The deeper I look inside myself, the worse it gets. I feel so much hate toward myself and at the bottom, I just feel empty. There is nothing, absolutely nothing.

MARRY - If I give you hug will you object?

- I do not need hugs. Thank you though. (She got up and took her plate filled with three pancakes and threw them away in the garbage.)

She went outside and sat on the front porch. The excitement turned into sadness. Her heart was dry, but her eyes and her face were wet. She was surrounded by fresh air, but she had difficulty breathing. She was not in jail, but she was imprisoned. She was not sick, but she was in pain.

145

She had money, but she was poor. She knew so many people, but she was lonely. And finally, she was breaking apart, but she was strong.

ALEX - I can't believe this.

- Good morning to you, too.

ALEX - Is this coincidence or what?

- Give me my milk, take your money and leave. (She took the money from her boot and handed it to him.) *Keep the change.*

ALEX - Obviously you wanted me here and now you're telling me to leave. It's very confusing. (He took the money and put it underneath one of the gallons.) My grandpa said to give you milk for free, but he wants a slice of cheese.

- (She smiled.) He is a nice man. Too bad he did not raise his grandson to be like him.

ALEX - Maybe I'm nicer than him. Why are you crying?

- Just feeling lonely in my new neighborhood.

ALEX - Don't worry, soon you will meet all great people in this town. How is your business going?

- It is dead. I closed it.

ALEX - Listen, you're kind of my neighbor now. If I can do anything for you, let me know. Welcome! (He extended his arm and she accepted his shake.)

- Thank you, AleX. Please say hello to MarviN.

146

She admired him while he was walking away. Of course, he was in a tight t-shirt as he was in the winter time. His muscles seemed even bigger and his short black hair was very shiny underneath the weak sunlight. His jeans covered his sneakers and they even reached the ground. There was something about his confident walk...

AleX reminded her of EdwarD!!! If she met EdwarD when he was in his twenties, she was sure he would have looked just like AleX.

She went back to the house. The money ended up back in her boots and the milk was placed in the fridge next to the other two gallons.

MarrY was folding her laundry in the living room and she decided to tell her about AleX later on. Now, she just wanted to post something on Facebook.

POST "RANDOM THOUGHTS" 64: *I do not get involved with a married man because I think I am better than his wife or because I think I am able to steal something that belongs to someone else. I do it because I think that I am not good enough to be in the first place in somebody's life. Being on the side, keeps my low self-esteem steady, and those leftovers of happiness that reach me, only when his sexual drive is high, are the only kind of happiness that grasps me. The marriage that I get involved with will never be broken, for a husband will never admit his cheating and the wife will never stand up for herself. When I am with a married man, everybody wins and gets what they want. The husband loves his wife and also he loves getting on the side something new and exciting. In marriage, wives get comfortable while husbands get bored. Wives are the ones who open the door for another woman to come and play with her husband. Every husband knows how far he can go with his wife and what will happen if he gets caught. Most of the wives blame a mistress for a husband's dishonesty. After one mistress there always comes another one.*

There are other kinds of marriages that I would not get involved with; a few smart wives in this country defend their family and their reputation by finding a way to make a husband feel pain for being unfaithful; by taking his kids, money and status away, just because he is a cheater. A man who loves his kids would never hurt their mother, for no child can be happy if mommy is sad. Most of the wives create even more pain for themselves by staying passive in the name of tradition, family and reputation. So, no, I do not feel sorry for them, because those wives choose to live with a cheater. That is one of the reasons why I do not want to take a place of a wife, because I do not want to lose all the privileges that mistresses have.

A married man comes to me with minimum expectations and he sees me as someone who is there to give him a good time. When a wife buys nice shoes to reward herself for her hard work, a husband gets himself a mistress as the reward. That is why he treats me so nice, because I am his luxury. I spend a short fun time with him and when the problems hit, he goes home. I do not see him when he is sick, tired, not showered, financially broke or depressed. Those moods belong to his wife. I see him when he is freshly groomed, excited, and ready to show his manhood by showing off financially, sexually, mentally and physically. Men are created to be driven by sex, and sex is with me, while wives take care of everything else.

***

In a few hours, her destiny will take the biggest spin so far. A new kind of misery will begin for her and she will not have control. Everything will be changed. She will be changed! Her biggest fear will become reality!

CHAPTER 20

PAST 8

Almost a week passed, and EdwarD did not visit or even call. Miss KellY complained a lot for being forgotten by her grandson.

That Thursday morning, she was pushing Miss KellY in her wheelchair through Central Park. It was cozy outside and a lot of people enjoyed various outside activities such as jogging, running, biking, and roller blading, but two of them managed to feel depressed on this energized day.

It was not only the fact that she was missing him so much that bothered her, but she also felt homesick, lonely, scared, bored, worthless and most of all; she felt empty unless EdwarD was around her.

KELLY - Let's take a break. Have a seat on this bench. (She parked Miss KellY's wheelchair next to the bench where she decided to lay down.)

- What Miss KellY, you feel tired from being pushed around?

KELLY - Very funny. Trust me, it is more tiring being in the same position for hours than to run around this park.

- How does it feel to be paralyzed?

KELLY - What kind of fucking question is that? It feels amazing and you should do it, too.

- Come on, you know what I mean. Do you get used to it? Does it bother you less with time? You seem unaffected by it. Why don't you get an electric chair?

KELLY - I can't put my pants or shoes on. I'm stuck in one place until someone moves me. I wear a diaper and I can't even wash my own ass. I'm a vegetable, but stronger than any dangerous animal on this planet. As long as I have my brain, I'll live a good life! When I stopped walking, I started crawling. My legs quit on me, but I hired women like you to be my legs. Do you think I became successful because I'm weak? No fucking way. I worked my way up and these legs never forced me to stop going toward my goals, they just made me change the path I was going. An electric chair is for lazy people who don't want to use their arms.

- I wish to be like you.

KELLY - Paralyzed?

- Strong, Miss KellY, strong! I am already paralyzed in my brain.

KELLY - Why do you say that?

- Because I am not smart.

KELLY - You'll not get pity from me. I don't feel sorry for people who can walk. If you feel stupid, that means you are.

- (She sarcastically smiled.) Do you think EdwarD sees me as a stupid woman?

KELLY - Ask him!

- *When is he coming?*

KELLY - I wish I knew. He must be busy fucking some ladies.

- *Does he do that?*

KELLY - Ask him if he fucks people around.

- *I cannot ask him that.*

KELLY - You can write him email.

- *How do you know?*

KELLY - Frankenstein and the Bible are missing from my shelves and I thought EdwarD took them, but he said he gave them to you and that you wrote interesting opinions.

- *Did he like them?*

KELLY - Cool off! We didn't speak about you in our entire phone conversation. We had more interesting things to talk about such as the stock market and my money.

- *I wish to see him again.*

KELLY - You know what you should do? Research his favorite painting and write him about it. You have plenty of time to waste, so waste it educationally.

- What should I research?

KELLY - The Painting called *White Crucifixion* by Marc Chagall.

- Why is that his favorite painting?

KELLY - Ask him! (She smiled.)

***

When evening came, she helped Miss KellY to take a bath and get ready for sleep. She spent hours reading online about Chagall and his work. Then she read many articles about *White Crucifixion*. Around midnight, she fell asleep.

Early in the morning, she decided to write an email to EdwarD. She hoped that Miss KellY would sleep a little bit longer, so she had enough time to organize her views.

From: green.card@hotmail.com
To: edward.NYC@gmail.com
Subject: White Crucifixion by Marc Chagall

Dear Mr. EdwarD,

Your grandma told me about your favorite painting and I decided to share my impression with you.

Please, feel free to comment… ;)

White Crucifixion - Painting by Marc Chagall

The picture of "White Crucifixion" was made in 1938 by the French artist, Marc Chagall. This artwork belongs to Modern and Contemporary Art. The material and technique used for the creation of this piece is oil on canvas.

The purpose of "White Crucifixion" was to promote wakefulness about Hitler's actions and their influences on all of mankind. "White Crucifixion" represents Jesus' suffering by the Jewish people.

Jesus, a Jewish man, is in the center of the art piece. Chagall used Biblical elements, but he gave them a new twist for his inspiration, as well as Hitler's politics toward Jewish people. "And they clothed him in a purple cloak; and after twisting some thorns into a crown, they put it on him (Mark 15:17)." Jesus on Chagall's picture is wearing a head-cloth instead of a crown made of thorns. "After mocking him, they stripped him of the purple cloak and put his own clothes on him (Mark 15:20)." Chagall dressed Jesus only in a Jewish prayer shawl around his waist. The halo around Jesus' head can be seen again around the Menorah which is located underneath his feet. The menorah is the symbol of Judaism. "You are to make a lampstand out of pure, hammered gold. It is to be made of one piece: its base and shaft, its ornamental cups, and its calyxes[a] and petals (Verse 32). Six branches are to extend from its sides, three branches of the lampstand from one side and three branches of the lampstand from the other side (Verse 33). There are to be three cups shaped like almond blossoms, each with a calyx and petals, on the first branch, and three cups shaped like almond blossoms, each with a calyx and petals, on the next branch. It is to be this way for the six branches that extend from the lampstand (Verse 34). There are to be four cups shaped like almond blossoms on the lampstand shaft along with its calyxes and petals (Verse 35). For the six branches that extend from the lampstand, a calyx must be under the first pair of branches from it, a calyx under the second pair of branches from it, and a calyx under the third pair of branches from it (Exodus 25:31-35)." Because all Jewish symbols are connected, the halo ties these two Jewish acquaintances.

All around the cross are elements of Judaism and modern Germany. The upper part of the painting is showing the persecution of Hebrew patriarchs in a smoke filled sky. In the upper right corner, is a soldier opening the door of a Torah ark on the fire, which was removed from the synagogue. The flag of Lithuania represents the root of Judaic learning. The mid-left side of the cross represents the story about refugees trying to escape on the ship from the burning village which was destroyed before the People's Army from the Soviet Union arrived. The arrival of the People's Army was inspired by Stalin's disapproval of Hitler's politics.

The ladder represents the symbol of God's promise to Jacob during his vision in Bethel. "I am with you and I will keep you wherever you go (Jacob 28:13-15)." The stream of smoke that is reaching the ladder is coming from the open Torah and going all the way up to Jesus. Did Chagall want to say that God's promises were gone like the smoke and only suffering was left for his chosen people?

At the bottom of the painting, the prophet Elijah, who is running away from Jesus, is shown giving the message that Jesus is not the messiah. The rest of the people are representing Jewish people running away from the crucifixion. All the people answered, "His blood be on us and on our children (Matthew 27:25.)" This verse was often used to express Jews' responsibility for Jesus' death.

I am not going to run away from this story. The "White Crucifixion" by Chagall is one of my favorite paintings ever, too. It is full of details, although complicated, can be seen and interpreted from many different angles, confusing and clear at the same time, and most of all, it is filled with so many different stories; this painting is just like the Bible. Sometimes, when I look at this picture, I can see a mini Bible being painted. It amazes me that the power of this work gives me new ideas each time when I look at Jesus, just like the Bible. If I am sad, Jesus looks to me like he is in pain and the smoke represents that God left him. But, when I need the courage in life, Jesus appears to me to be in peace. The smoke represents the Holy Spirit which is coming to take Jesus to a much better place. The Bible and the "White Crucifixion" will never lose the ability to give me something new each time I visit them.

REFERENCES:

1)   The Holy Bible
2)   The AMICA Library
http://www.davidrumsey.com/amica/amico249474-5325.html
3)   White Crucifixion -Painting by Marc Chagall
http://www.wikipaintings.org/en/marc-chagall/white-crucifixion-1938

... Mr. EdwarD, your grandma misses you so much all these days. Please, come visit her. Please, please, please...

BarbiE

She was braiding her hair in front of the mirror in the living room when she heard the front door being unlocked.

EDWARD - Hi BarbiE! Are you busy?

- Mr. EdwarD, your grandma is watching a movie. She will be so happy when she sees you.

EDWARD - I came to speak to you.

- Sure, you seem serious. (Her heart was beating too fast.)

She left her hair alone and sat on the couch.

- I am listening.

EDWARD - I'm a lawyer so I tend to have a certain approach to problems. This time, I'll make an exception. (He sat next to her on the couch.) I will be straight forward. BarbiE, you're spending way too much of your precious time on me. There is no need to write me mile-long emails every few days.

- Are you mad at me?

Her body was shaking. She was squeezing her gloved fingers and the preexisting pain become stronger, but the aching in her heart was dominating.

EDWARD - Don't worry how I feel. BarbiE, I don't represent any value in your life. I'm not worth your time. Invest all your energy in yourself and of course in my grandma, but not in me.

157

- Are my emails bad?

EDWARD - I hate literature. To me, everything is the same, because I don't care to understand it. Ask my mother... She'll tell you, and prove to you what the right perspective is.

- Why is Marc Chagall your favorite artist?

EDWARD - (He laughed.) He's not! I don't have a favorite artist. I don't understand art either. My grandma thinks that she'll go to hell because she doesn't have a religion so she wants me to belong somewhere. That painting is in my hallway because it was a gift from her. You researched all that information for nothing. I don't care!

- I apologize for wasting your time.

EDWARD - Don't waste it any longer. I'm sorry if I confused you with my behavior.

- No, I am the one who misinterpreted the situations. Thank you for being straightforward. (She was about to get up and leave.)

EDWARD - BarbiE, you are such a special girl. You are so beautiful, intelligent, caring, and hard-working. You have all the tools needed for success.

- Of course I do. (She said with sarcasm.) *And you believe in those words.*

EDWARD - I strongly believe it, but you are the one who has to accept it as true, so you can move forward. BarbiE, what is your ultimate goal?

- *I do not have one. I am surviving day-by-day.*

EDWARD - Is my grandma that bad that you have to survive around her? (He laughed.)

- *Miss Kelly is one of the best things that ever came into my life. My response was in general.*

EDWARD - Where did you learn to speak English and why are you so interested in writing?

- *Thank you for not being harsh on my English skills. (She smiled.) At least not right now.*

EDWARD - When I ask you a question, I expect an answer. (He demanded.)

- *My stepmother always wanted to escape the country, so she learned English as a young girl. When she moved in my house, she bonded with me through reading and teaching. She taught me English as much as she knew, and the rest I taught myself by reading books. I liked to believe that reading books made me smarter. (*She took a deep breath.)

EDWARD - That is what books are supposed to do. In your case, it worked.

- *I wish it was true. How about you, Mr. EdwarD? How did you become so smart?*

EDWARD - I was born smart. (He chuckled.)

- *I believe that.* (She said seriously.)

EDWARD - No, BarbiE, everybody is born dumb.
Today I'm considered smart, thanks to a certain amount
of investment in my potential.

- *What? Miss KimberlY injected you with some smart
genes?*

EDWARD - If that would exist, I would be filled with it
on a daily basis. My mother and my grandmother saw
me as their project that was supposed to be worked on
forever.

- *Lucky you!*

EDWARD - Lucky? Maybe, I don't know any other
kind of parenting, but this one didn't bring me
happiness.

- *At least you were raised under parenting dogma.*

EDWARD - Parenting dogma? (He chuckled.) The worst
thing that my mother put me though was gymnastics. I
hated it so much. I wanted to do karate but my mother
was too scared that I might get hurt. Luckily, I broke my
leg doing gymnastics when I was seven and she never
sent me back. Gymnastics became too dangerous for my
well-being.

- *She loves you so much.*

EDWARD - She does and she controls me so much, too. As a teenager, I was allowed to have friends and dates only if I would spend my time with them in my house. I bet you she had cameras all over the house, so she could see everything that I do.

- No, she did not. She does not love you that much. (She giggled.)

EDWARD – Oh, yes, she does! Sometimes hating and loving too much brings the same outcome.

- Tell me about your dad. I never met him.

EDWARD - My dad is my mother's toy. He only does what she tells him to do. Growing up, I was scared of my mother, but I knew that my father was even more scared of her.

- Do you love your mother?

EDWARD - Very much! She's an amazing woman who can't be stopped in any way. She's loving, strong, successful, a fighter and most of all; she's always right. She's an outstanding attorney and she will make a great judge as soon as my father launches his political career.

- I wish them both a lot of luck.

EDWARD - I wish you the best luck possible, young lady. I'm telling you, as a father figure, to set up some goals and work toward them. Continue reading what you like and write beautiful emails to yourself.

- You will not start ignoring me, right?

EDWARD - Why would I do such a thing? It is my pleasure to be around you. Remember BarbiE, you must forget me. (He got up from the couch, quickly touched her face and left.)

She slowly lifted her heavy body, carrying a broken heart, and she walked toward the hallway to Miss KellY's room. Miss KellY was sitting in her wheelchair at the entrance of the hallway.

- Do you need anything, Miss KellY?

KELLY - I needed to be changed, but I didn't dare to interrupt your conversation.

- I will help you get cleaned now.

KELLY - He didn't even bother to ask you about his fucking grandma.

- One time someone didn't care about you. My entire life no one cared about me.

KELLY - And don't you fucking dare to think that EdwarD does. PrincesS, listen to me, he'll never give you what you need.

- I'm worthless. What do I do to make him like me? (She burst into tears and sat in front of Miss KellY's wheelchair.)

KELLY - Open your Facebook account and write all of your crappy essays there. You don't need EdwarD to read them. You'll find plenty of weird people as weird as you are who might enjoy reading them. If a man ever makes you cry that means you should run away from him as fast as you can.

Two weeks passed, and she never heard from him. Miss KellY met with him in KimberlY's house over a family dinner.

She was alone in the apartment and she decided to open her Facebook account. After a few minutes, she was ready for her first post.

POST "RANDOM THOUGHTS" 1: *How can it be explained? How? Well, it is just an urge. The same urge as to drink when you are thirsty or to sleep when you are tired. I just need to see him, to be around him under any kind of circumstances. It does not matter if he is nice or mean to me, as long as he acknowledges me. Just the feeling that he knows that I exist, is the promise that maybe one day he might love me. Even though, I know, I see, and even feel that he does not want me, he does not like me, and he is not enjoying my presence, I still have the hope that if I change myself, he will change the way he feels about me. If I become a little bit prettier, smarter, or funnier, then he might fall in love with me. Oh, my dear God, even though I know it will never work between him and I, just because he is way out of my reach, I still have a hope. I am just asking for a small amount of his attention toward me. What do I do? How do I make him love me? Or at least, how do I make myself stop loving him? Or, finally how do I kill the hope of having him? I love him, because he is so much above me. He is perfect, way too perfect when I look at all his imperfections.*

CHAPTER 21

PAST 9

Miss KellY became quieter and less talkative. KimberlY visited more often than ever before because she was wondering why her mother suddenly changed. EdwarD stopped coming to Miss KellY's place. She sent back home enough money for her stepmother, sister and little brother to go to the capital and place him in the hospital for testing. She just lived like a statue, without attempting to make a step forward.

That morning, she changed Miss KellY's diaper without even speaking to her. Then she made a breakfast only for Miss KellY and then left to her room. Miss KellY found her hysterically crying on top of her bed.

KELLY - What the fuck is wrong with you?

- I experienced different rejections and I am used to being treated like worthless garbage. None of that hurts me this much. What bothers me the most is that he was good to me and I ruined it. I am the one who pushed him away. I am the one who jumped too high. I forgot that I was nobody. How could I even dare to think that he would ever be with me?

KELLY - What the fuck do you want from him?

- I just want him next to me. When he is next to me, I feel alive.

KELLY - You're enchanted by him and you're imagining what he is, without truly understanding who he is.

- He is perfect.

164

KELLY - He's a 40-year-old single man, who looks like a four month pregnant woman, and he's a selfish fuck who knows how to charm every vagina in this city with his bullshit talk and his family's money.

- None of that matters to me, besides the fact that he was so good to me.

KELLY - You are truly a stupid woman! Men are supposed to be good to women all the time. If you fuck him, would you feel better?

- Miss KellY, we are talking about your grandson.

KELLY - And you, too. I care about you, you stupid girl.

She got up from the bed and hugged Miss KellY's legs.

- God bless you for all your kindness.

KELLY - Enough now! (Miss KellY pointed with her finger to go back onto the bed.) Do you want to fuck him or not?

- He does not want to touch me.

KELLY - I was 15 years old when I gave birth to KimberlY. I am from Colorado and my family never talked to me about sex. My boyfriend was 17 years old and I was 14. We watched adult movies and we decided to try it. Our curiosity produced a present called "KimberlY". I moved to New York so I could provide more for my baby than just a poor life. When she became a teenager, I told her everything about sex, hoping she would never have children at a young age. When she turned 15, she gave birth to EdwarD. She did it on purpose because she wanted to hurt me. I decided not to allow EdwarD to continue the family pattern of

165

having children at a young age and suffer like me and my daughter. KimberlY and I agreed for the first time ever and we controlled EdwarD. I guess we controlled him too much. He's 40 and has no wife or kids. It doesn't matter what is done in this family, somehow at the end, we all end up fucked up in one way or the other.

- Thank you for telling me, but how is knowing all this going to help me with EdwarD?

KELLY - It won't, but it helped me saying it. And it's connected to sex. (She laughed.) Let's go back to you and my grandson.

- How do I get his attention?

KELLY - Since man existed, the oldest trick never failed. You get and keep a man through sex.

- Does it work with EdwarD?

KELLY - Unless he's become gay. If you sleep with him, are you going to stop being fucking depressed?

- If he ever kisses me, I will blossom like a butterfly.

KELLY - Butterflies don't blossom you stupid woman. Obviously, not even basic science is your field.

- Let's go back to EdwarD! What do I do Miss KellY?

KELLY - I'll take out some clothes from my closet, the ones I wore when I was a" man hunter". I'll put some make up on you and fix your hair. Basically, I'll transform you and you'll be changed into a butterfly or "blossomed" like one. (She giggled.)

- Butterflies bring bad memories to me.

KELLY - Why did you mention them then? You like hurting yourself for some reason. Enough about fucking flying animals! Listen, I'll tell him that I'm coming to visit him tonight and you'll take it from there.

- *Can you come?*

KELLY - And do what? What kind of romance includes an old lady in a wheelchair?

- *Mine does. I would be really glad to have a dinner with you and him.*

KELLY - Sweetie, you're going there to eat but not dinner. Use your imagination and seduce the man. That is as hard as forcing a frog to jump into water.

***

The tall, skinny, blonde girl, wearing a tight red dress which barely covered her bottom, entered into the building on Park Ave. She was wearing gold sandals which were out-shined by her long simmering legs. Her gold pedicure balanced well with her large, golden hoop earrings. Her hair was straight and it reached the end of her back. Her green eyes were even greener because of the black mascara and eyeliner surrounding them. Her lips were covered with many layers of pink lip gloss. Her hands were covered with gold gloves. In one hand, she was carrying a gold and red clutch and in the other, a covered bowl containing seafood salad.

She said a short prayer in her head and then she knocked at his penthouse door. The receptionist already announced her arrival. He opened the door.

EDWARD - Holy!... (He looked at her surprised and stood silently.)

He was wearing blue pajama bottoms and a sleeveless black undershirt. She realized that he actually was kind of a muscular man. Even with his imperfect body, he was still perfectly sexy. His short black hair was still wet from the shower.

EDWARD - Look at you BarbiE doll! Where are you going tonight?

- *Good evening, Mr. EdwarD. Miss KellY could not make it, for she wanted to rest after a long day. She sent me to bring you seafood salad. It is made with the imitation of crab meat so it is vegan.*

EDWARD - Would you like to come in for a minute? Sorry, I'm not properly dressed. I was in the shower so I grabbed the first thing that crossed my path.

- *I would like to come inside.*

She walked inside his place. The left side of the small entrance hallway was decorated with the *White Crucifixion* painting. The large room was divided into a kitchen with a bar, and a living space with two large sofas facing each other. A small coffee table was between them. The biggest amount of space belonged to a gigantic black piano.

EDWARD - It looks cool, right?

- *It is a beautiful place.*

EDWARD - Come see this. (He took the bowl from her hands and placed it on the bar. Then he walked quickly toward the spiral stair case leading to the inner balcony.)

She climbed up the stairs and she could not believe her eyes. His oval bed, larger than a king size, was on the right side of the huge open room. The Jacuzzi, as big as a queen size mattress, was on the opposite side of the bed. Next to the Jacuzzi, were two doors. One was leading to a bathroom and the other to a walk-in closet. Just by sitting on the bed, the entire living room area could be seen from above. The penthouse did not have any windows but plenty of light was coming in through the glass roof. It was magical. It reminded her of a box covered with crystal.

- *This entire space is breathtaking.*

EDWARD - I have a unique taste, young lady.

- *Yes, you do.*

EDWARD - In everything, young lady.

- *Stop calling me that.*

EDWARD - I have to remind myself that there is a huge age gap between us. Otherwise I would get carried away.

- *Maybe I want you to be carried away.*

EDWARD - Is that why you came? To come into my unique world?

- *I came to bring you the food that Miss KellY made.*

EDWARD - BarbiE, listen to me. Since the day she moved to New York, your Miss KellY never cut her own meat on her plate. She never even thought about cooking something. I think she doesn't even know how to mix the soup inside of her bowl.

- Then why do you think I came, Mr. EdwarD?

EDWARD - I am scared to guess.

He walked downstairs and sat on one of his bar stools. She followed him down and then she sat on top of the piano. He turned toward her.

EDWARD - It's funny how women imagine that making love on the piano is romantic. It's very painful and uncomfortable.

- If I tried it, I could tell you my opinion.

EDWARD - BarbiE, be careful what you're wishing for.

- When we met for the first time, you told me that you were looking forward to play games with me. Remember?

EDWARD - I remember very well our last conversation. (He emphasized the word "last".)

- I do not. I am sure it was not very interesting to me. Can you amuse me in some other way so I can remember our time spent together?

EDWARD - I wish to know how.

- Yes, you do. You just have to follow your instincts.

He smiled uncomfortably and then he walked toward her, and placed his palm on her cheek.

- Why do you do that? Even before, you touched my face like that.

EDWARD - I like to feel the heat coming from your rosy cheeks.

- You know, you are more than welcome to find other warm places.

EDWARD - No BarbiE, that is a very appealing idea, but not a smart one.

She grabbed his face with her hands and placed her lips on his. He did not give her passion in return. He moved away from her and opened the front door.

EDWARD - Please, leave! I am begging you to leave.

- No, Mr. EdwarD. I am not going away until I get what I want. You can leave and when you come back, you will find me here, or you can stay and enjoy the show.

She got off the piano and walked toward the stairs. She took off her shoes and unzipped her dress. While she was walking up the stairs, her dress fell off of her body. Her bare back side was turned to him.

- Oh, Mr. EdwarD, it seems I forgot to wear any underwear.

Before she even reached the bed, he swiftly ran up the stairs and came behind her. He grabbed her from the back and pushed her onto it.

EDWARD - BarbiE, you're the one asking for this. You still have time to make a move. (His black eyes stared into her green eyes.)

- I will make a move once you are inside me.

He stripped off his undershirt and sweatpants. He wasn't wearing underwear either. His masculinity reached its potential.

His naked body was on top of hers. He placed a first wet kiss on her eye and then slowly, he placed his lips close to hers, but he waited some time before he slipped his tongue inside of her mouth. His full lips were locked with her glossy lips. He was taking short breaks to catch heavy, much-needed breaths. She felt his heart beating rapidly on the top of her breasts.

He slowly moved his body next to her, locked his fingers with hers, and with the other hand, he was going through her hair.

EDWARD - If I do this to you, then I'll do it the right way. Meet me in front of the piano.

He jumped off the bed and ran down the stairs. She quickly pranced to the bathroom and looked at herself in the mirror. Miss KellY made her look like a real Barbie doll. On the way down, she just put her shoes on. She covered her breast with her hair.

He opened the bottle of Chateau Ausone, Saint-Emilion Grand Cru, France wine on the piano after he poured it into two glasses. Then, he placed his naked body in front of the black and white keys. She was standing in front of him wearing only shoes and gloves.

EDWARD - My favorite composer, ever, is Frank Sinatra. I never played him on this piano for anyone, because I waited for someone deserving of that privilege. I'm going to play for you *The Way You Look Tonight* by him. For my father, I play Bach, for my mother, Mozart and for my grandma, Beethoven. There is a reason why each of you inspires me to play a specific composer. Now you have some research to do. (He winked at her.)

He started to play the composition passionately. Her eyes were filled with happy tears and she enjoyed every second of it. Her perfect EdwarD knew how to play the instrument. It felt so natural being nude in front of him. When the song came to an end, she sat on his lap and hugged him.

- Thank you for being so good to me. You make me feel very happy.

EDWARD - I'll make you feel other emotions, too. All night is reserved for a grown-up play date.

- Please, Mr. EdwarD, play with me any way you want and as long as you desire.

EDWARD - You know, I would be crazy if I were to pass on that offer.

He passed her the glass of wine and before he took his own, she placed her glass back on the piano and put his hands on her legs.

- I will teach you how to drink.

She tilted his head back with her left hand, and started pouring the wine from the bottle slowly into his mouth with her other hand. As soon as some wine started dripping down his chin, she quickly caught it with her tongue and then she placed her lips on his. They shared the rest of the wine inside his mouth.

- Now it is your turn to drink.

She stood up and started pouring the wine on her shoulder. It took a path over her left breast, and then it reached her belly. She leaned to the side so it could keep pouring over her private area. He looked at her with excitement in his eyes and then placed his lips down there and started licking the wine which was slowly coming down her body.

When the bottle was empty, he licked all the way up, tracing the path backwards. His lips crossed her belly, then circled around her breast, then quickly placed a few soft kisses on her shoulder. He then passionately kissed her lips, fast, and even faster. For a while, neither of them was able to breathe.

He took her by the hand and they rushed upstairs onto the bed. Due to the testosterone rush, he forgot about his intentions of being a gentleman and he rushed to feel inside of her. His main focus was enjoying her now and as fast as he could. Her wetness and her synchronized movements gave him a motive to continue with his rhythm. Lying on top of her gave him absolute control, which he could not handle for long.

After he reached his orgasm, he placed his head on her flat stomach, facing her, which imprinted a terror in his mind. He jumped as fast as he could, ran to the bathroom and put on a blue robe. He took a box of tissues and a large white towel.

EDWARD - What did I do to you?

He sat her up and covered her with a towel. With tissues, he wiped her tears.

EDWARD - Please talk to me.

- I am sorry.

EDWARD - I'm the one who should be apologizing. I completely forgot about you and I treated you like a...

(He paused). I didn't care about you or your pleasure, I just...

- ...*It is okay. I do not mind. I ruined this night.* (She started crying loudly.)

EDWARD - BarbiE, you did nothing wrong, I assure you. Please tell me what I can do to make you stop crying?

- *Hug me tight and hold me in your arms like you care about me.*

He laid flat on the mattress and positioned her body on top of his. He hugged her with one arm and with the other, he was patting her hair like she was a little baby resting on his chest.

Knowing what was going through her mind, I felt pain, if that was possible. There she was, getting moments of love which will end up being too emotionally expensive. She rushed tonight, as many times before, to obtain the attention, and she succeeded only after she offered her body. And then, only her body mattered, not her. This happened before and it will happen again until she improves her low self-esteem.

EDWARD - What are you thinking about?

- *Many times, I imagined being in your arms. My imagination was not near as good as this reality.*

EDWARD - Now, you make me feel good.

- *I want to make you feel good always.*

EDWARD - BarbiE, why do you feel so strongly about me?

175

- Mr. EdwarD, you are...

EDWARD - No more Mr.! I think we passed our formal relationship.

- Fine, EdwarD! (She smiled.) You are so nice to me and you care about me.

EDWARD - You have parents, right?

- I have a younger sister, way younger half-brother and a step-mother.

EDWARD - Tell me about your childhood.

- I was a child, but I never had a child's life.

EDWARD - Where are your biological parents?

- To me, they do not exist and I do not want to speak about them.

EDWARD - Do you have any family in the US?

- Yes I do, Miss KellY and you.

EDWARD - (He smiled.) You really became attached to my grandma.

- And to her grandson. (She touched his face with her hand covered with a gold glove.)

EdwarD continued playing with her hair and with the other han,; he took her hand away from his face and placed it close to his heart.

EDWARD - I respect your choice to hide your past, but if you ever decide to show what is inside, (he kissed her glove) my grandma and I will support you. And I'm not only speaking about your covered hands.

- Why are you so nice to me?

EDWARD - You deserve from everyone to be nice to you.

- Why do you think that?

EDWARD - You are kind, hardworking, and respectful; you want to make whoever is around you happy. Not only should your oracle be in the Bible, but people should write about you in it, because you are a saint.

- Now you are going to extremes.

EDWARD - Extremes are good. They make life worth living.

- Your grandma will kill me for staying out this late.

EDWARD - If she needs you, she would have called you by now. She is not a shy lady.

- Definitely not. Do you want me to leave?

EDWARD - I'm never letting you go. We'll get up and go eat some of that seafood salad that "my grandma made for me".

(Both laughed.)

- It was her idea to tell you that lie.

EDWARD - Don't take all the advice that she gives you.

- Thanks to her, I am here. Can we skip eating and stay in the bed until morning?

EDWARD - You're very hard to please, my BarbiE.

177

- Stop with your sarcasm. Take off your robe. I want to feel your body again.

EDWARD - It's easier to control myself if I'm not in direct contact with your warm skin.

- Who said you need to control yourself?

EDWARD - After what happened tonight, I have to. I'm not going to make you cry again. Not in that way, anyway.

- Give me a second chance.

EDWARD - Maybe later on, if you desire, both of us can get another chance.

Hours passed quickly. He was sleeping and she was wide awake, admiring his tanned complexion, full lips, and his dark hair. She gently placed kisses all over his sleeping body. Or at least, she thought he was deep asleep.

CHAPTER 22

That evening, she and MarrY were boiling milk for cheese. She was thrilled that she managed to have a normal conversation with AleX. She was looking forward to seeing him again.

Suddenly, both women heard someone walking outside. She went to her room to take her gun, while MarrY casually decided to open the door and check who was outside. When she came back downstairs, a big surprise was waiting for her.

MARRY - This handsome man is looking for you.

- *How did you find me, DaxoN?*

MARRY - Oh my goodness.

DAXON - Why did you put me in a position to look for you?

- *What do you want?*

DAXON - I want his full name, address and phone number.

- *I cannot do that. I have to protect him and his family.*

DAXON - I'm protecting you while you're protecting others. What is in it for me?

MARRY - Dear DaxoN, maybe you should leave and come back another time.

- *How did you find me?*

DAXON - This woman (he pointed at MarrY) called me and told me to come and take you away.

MARRY - Never! You're such a liar...

- *MarrY, don't worry! DaxoN, how did you find me?*

DAXON - Your AleX gave me directions to this house. I found you thanks to him.

- *Okay. Thank you for your visit. You can leave now.*

DAXON - I am asking you for the last time to give me his information.

- *And I am refusing it for the last time.*

DAXON - Today is the last time in many things for you. Can you please walk me out?

- *My pleasure.*

She opened the door for DaxoN and she followed him outside. MarrY was behind them. The night was very close; the darkness of her life was even closer.

Suddenly, police officers started making a visible circle around the house. Each second more and more officers appeared.

- *What is this, DaxoN?*

DAXON - Sorry boss, I have to follow justice. The sex tapes in DevY's house were found and I didn't have difficulty recognizing you on them. It seems you have had a lot of fun with your husband and his two friends.

(She took a gun out of her pocket and pointed at him.)

POLICE OFFICER - Put the gun down! Put your hands in the air and lie down on the ground! I'm "Officer DrakE", one of DevY's best friends.

MarrY was hysterically crying. DaxoN was standing proud. She felt nothing. Her gun was dropped to the ground, her hands were raised in the air, and her mind became frozen in order for her to stay protected.

Everything was moving too fast. She was pushed to the ground by a few officers. They handcuffed her after they had beaten her body. They called her all kinds of names and pulled her toward the police cars that were parked on the road. Grass and dirt found a way to her mouth where it was mixed with blood. DaxoN was still standing proud and MarrY was yelling at police officers.

The immigration prisons are owned and operated by the Department of Homeland Security, local state city jails, and private prisons. All of them are paid by ICE (Immigration and Customs Enforcement) to house those considered deportable. ICE pays local jails around $95 per day, per person. The average price of keeping an immigrant prisoner is only $20 per day and if a jail skimps on requirements such as food and health care, it can increase its profit.

She was taken to The Buffalo Federal Detention Facility in New York which holds around 360 immigration inmates. Because this specific facility does not have a wing for women, she was placed in a section which served as a holding area. Shortly after her arrival, she was being questioned by four men, all of them in civilian clothes.

DRAKE - State your full name and date of birth.

- *I do not have an identity.*

DRAKE - This is not time to fool around. Who really are you?

- It might be hard proving to the entire world who I really am, but it is not as hard as proving it to myself.

DRAKE - You are not cooperating. Here is a short summary for you. DevY was my best friend for years and you are responsible for his murder. I will be involved in your case until I make sure you suffered three times more than him. First, I will make sure that justice gets satisfied here and then I'll deport your ass to whichever country you came from.

- Did you see the videos?

DRAKE - You are obviously so proud of them. Sorry honey, none of us want to fuck you.

- Did you see what kind of monster he was?

DRAKE - We don't know that and we are not getting involved in your sex life with your husband.

- He abused me!

DRAKE - Sure he did, maybe you are the one who asked to play those kinds of kinky games and he just did you a favor out of love. By the way, those videos are gone, so the judge will think that you're bluffing.

- This is the end for me in every sense, right?

DRAKE - This is the beginning of the end for you.

Another man pushed her out of the office and locked her in the small storage-like room. There was no bed, or blanket or even a toilet bowl. It looked like it was a closet under renovation. She could even smell fresh paint. It was dark and cold. She lied down on the cement floor and closed her eyes. Warm blood was leaving her face, her limbs, and some was coming out of her mouth. She knew she was bruised all over. None of this hurt her as much as reality did. Life with DevY, ups and downs with EdwarD, Miss KellY's death, constant hiding, homesickness, her little sister, the death of her brother, and finally, her incarceration. She is about to be deported; her biggest fear became reality! Or at least, she believed that was her biggest terror.

***

The following morning, she was taken out of the room and brought to the bathroom by a female officer who stayed with her the entire time. Her jeans were wet from slow, painful urinating during the night. She took off her jeans and shirt, rinsed them out and placed them on the floor until she wiped her body with wet toilet paper. Then she put her clothes back on and folded her hair in a bun. She looked at the mirror and saw a skinny, bruised, pale face, with a cut lip and lifeless eyes. From there, she was brought to a phone. She dialed EdwarD's cellphone number and she was connected to his voicemail.

- *EdwarD, I am in The Buffalo Federal Detention Facility. I do not know what to do. I am scared. I am scared a lot.*

She was escorted back to the room where she spent the night. On the floor, was a plastic plate with a peanut and butter jelly sandwich. For hours, she was standing frozen. The same woman from the morning came to escort her in the visiting area because someone came to see her.

She was feeling calmer knowing that EdwarD was there and he would tell her what to do. In a large area with tables and chairs, she found AleX, sitting down at the table. She approached and sat across from him. She was not disappointed, but not glad either.

ALEX - What did they do to you? (He looked at her bloody face and torn clothes.)

- Why did you give DaxoN my address?

ALEX - I met him at your bar and I got the impression that he was your friend. When he came to my house, he said that he had difficulties finding your new home, because the GPS couldn't locate it and I told him how to get there. I never knew that you were running away from him until MarrY came to my house, ready to kill me, and told me what happened.

- How is she?

ALEX - Running around like crazy not knowing how to help you.

- There is no help for me.

ALEX - Then all together we will find something. MarrY put her house up for sale today, so she can pay the best lawyer for your case. My grandpa and I are going to invest our savings also.

- No AleX, thank you all. There is no help for me. It is the end. But I need a favor from you.

ALEX - Tell me.

- I need you to contact EdwarD. In MarrY's house, in my bedroom, is my black backpack. There is EdwarD's information, printed bank statements, and some cash in it. Find him and tell him to sponsor my sister's student visa so she can enter the country. When she arrives here, tell him to open the bank account in her name and transfer all of my money into it.

ALEX - Does he have your sister's address?

- *Just give him my entire backpack after you find a way to get to him. My sister's address is inside.*

ALEX - I'll do it tomorrow morning. I just put some money in your account in here so you can pay for phone calls, buy some clothes and food.

- *Thank you. The money in that backpack should be shared between you and MarrY.*

ALEX - MarrY can keep it. Listen, you can count on me. You can!

- *Thank you.*

Before he left, he gently hugged her and promised her that he will make sure that EdwarD does what she said to be done.

***

Two days later, nothing changed. She was wearing the same clothes, her blood clotted, and DrakE threatened her as he did the first night. She was still in the same room and the first sandwich was still there. The female officer told her that she would not get another one until she finished the first one because this place does not like to waste food.

Today, she asked to visit the store after her bathroom visit. In the store, she purchased a pen and notebook. Before she exited, the solution for all of her problems appeared: duct tape. She bought two of them. As soon as she arrived back to her room, she started writing even though she could not see the lines on the paper.

185

"My loving baby sister, please forgive me for not succeeding in this life. I loved you since you were born, until the moment I died and I promise I will love you beyond that. My angel, reach your goals for both of us and stay strong no matter where your life takes you. You can trust a man named EdwarD, who will help you reach your goals. I love you so much, I love you too much. I did not have another choice. Even though I am a bad person, I am still able to love you so much. All of these years passed, but I can still remember the smell of your hair and I can still feel the softness of your skin. I love you my angel. "

On the other paper she wrote *"EdwarD, I am begging you to take care of my sister. Bring her here and give her my money. Keep some for yourself and give the rest to her. Thank you!"*

She left the notebook on the side. She opened the duct tape and started wrapping it around her head by covering her entire nose including her nostrils. The other tape was about to cover her mouth.

Suddenly, I saw nothing but darkness. I could not see her future anymore. It was gone. I could not feel her emotions. It seemed she was empty, and therefore, I became, too. If I don't come out, she will cover her mouth and she will stop breathing. I will reach highs and she will be lost forever. If I come out, I will be lost, but she might have a chance of escaping black endlessness. I have to choose between myself and her.

CHAPTER 23

PAST 10

She left the bed and walked downstairs to get some water from the fridge. Inside, she found a can of whipped cream. While she looked for a spoon, she got an idea. The night before, EdwarD gave her the emotional support that she needed and there was only one way to thank a man for his kindness.

She went upstairs and sneaked back into his bed. His robe was already opened. She poured the cream on his chest, belly and made a "whipped cream mountain" on the top of his masculinity.

EDWARD - What are you doing?

- Eating.

EDWARD - Does this mean I'm about to find out how it feels to be a plate?

- You are about to find out how it feels to be a lollipop.

She licked off all the cream around his body and when she reached his private area, the mountain was raised even higher. She licked all the sweetness off his masculinity and then sucked it as if it was a lollipop filled with the most delicious juice. His breathing signaled that he was about to reach the top of his "pleasure" mountain. After he filled her mouth with delicious contents, she swallowed everything. They cuddled for a while and then she went back to Miss KellY's place.

Months were passing quickly and her attachment for EdwarD grew. She was writing happy thoughts on her Facebook. Miss KellY wanted to do another Botox, so she asked her to accompany her to various doctors' visits.

She took care of Miss KellY the entire day and cared for EdwarD the entire night. Many nights he spent in his grandma's apartment, playing with his BarbiE.

Occasionally, he emailed her the time and the name of a hotel where he waited for her filled with excitement. Sometimes, he would have costumes and toys ready for role-play. He was living in a reality where all his fantasies were coming to life with a woman who asked for nothing and gave everything.

Even though their sex life was filled with unpredictable, but passionate acts, she felt that their relationship was more than just sex. In the meantime, she opened herself to him and told him some of her regrets. It felt great sharing her emotional load with someone. He learned that she was a prostitute before she entered the country, worked as a stripper and that she was married and she left her abusive husband. He did not judge her. In the future, she planned to tell him about the murders, too.

***

He accompanied her on a shopping trip for the people overseas and he enjoyed wrapping presents for people that he never met. When he received her sister's email inspired by gratitude, he felt that he was losing his selfish side. Her little brother was a reason why he went shopping for Legos, cars and toy guns. He couldn't wait to meet her family, the one that he helped so much without even knowing them.

After today's doctor's visit, Miss KellY was crying.

- What happened?

KELLY - Nothing.

- I will keep asking you until you tell me.

KELLY - I can't do any more Botox. Fucking doctor said that my skin is stretched to the maximum.

- It looks like that. How much Botox should a woman get in her life? Isn't that a one-time thing?

KELLY - Forget it! Tonight we are going in KimberlY's house for dinner. This will be the best thing that I ever did for you.

- Why? I do not feel like going. You go and be with your family.

KELLY - You want to be part of the family, so come tonight and see what you were missing for the last few months while you were fucking around with EdwarD.

- Whatever you want, Miss KellY.

***

Miss KellY looked very elegant in her navy blue dress and black heels. Her black hair was put up in a bun. KimberlY's dining room was on the second floor and Miss KellY was brought up in a service elevator. Miss KellY called each of the guests by name and all of them, one after another, came to give her a hug. Altogether, there were KimberlY, her husband JohN, Dr.

DaN, his wife ElissA, EdwarD, and MelanY. As soon as they finished hugging and greeting each other, Miss KellY took a filled wine glass from the table without knowing who it belonged to. All of them ignored her inappropriate act.

Dr. DaN briefly shook the hand of a girl who was standing behind the wheelchair. Miss Kelly realized that, for some reason, her private companion made everyone in the room a little bit uncomfortable.

KELLY - For some of you who don't know this gorgeous girl, this is PrincesS, my family member. She is beautiful outside, but she is even prettier inside.

(Everyone greeted her with a polite smile.)

KIMBERLY - Mother please, go to the head of the table where you have enough space for your chair. Your PrincesS can go in the kitchen and wait there.

KELLY - No, she will sit next to me.

KIMBERLY - Mother, please. Let's celebrate tonight as a family.

DAN - I don't mind if KellY's assistant joins us.

ELISSA - I am sure you don't, but KimberlY is right, this is a family dinner.

MELANY - Are we going to spend this evening discussing guest arrangement or celebrate?

KIMBERLY - MelanY darling, you are right, we are here tonight to celebrate your and EdwarD's engagement.

As an invisible ghost, crying invisible tears, she stepped out of the room and went into the kitchen. She was trying to process everything at once: EdwarD's coldness, humiliation, engagement, DaN's niceness, and most of all, the acknowledgement that Miss KellY stood up for her. The silence in the kitchen and the noise in her head were broken by EdwarD's voice.

EDWARD - Why didn't you tell me that you are coming to the dinner?

- I did not know either. Your grandma made me come, last minute.

EDWARD - Now the crazy woman tells you what to do?

- Do not speak like that about your grandma. You are only mad that I saw you with her.

EDWARD - Listen, MelanY and I are getting married.

- What are you and I doing?

EDWARD - There is no "us", BarbiE. Don't you dare say anything to MelanY or anybody else in here.

- What is there to say? You said that I am no one to you.

EDWARD - I'll come to grandma's apartment later and we'll talk. Control your emotions and don't come upstairs. I'll bring grandma down to you when we're done.

- Yes, Mr. Edward.

EDWARD - Don't try to act clever.

Two hours later, EdwarD and MelanY brought Miss Kelly into the kitchen. This time, she took a few minutes to admire EdwarD's fiancé. She was a fuller woman in all the right places. Her large breasts and huge behind made her tiny waist even smaller. She had curly brown hair up to her shoulders. She was wearing a tight brown dress up to her knees. Her heels were sky high. Judging by her complexion, she assumed that she must be of mixed race. Her walk was confident and she carried herself like she owned the world.

MELANY - My name is" MelanY". (She extended her well-manicured hand towards her and she accepted it with her hand, covered with a black glove.)

- Nice to meet you, Miss MelanY.

MELANY - Just MelanY is fine. I would like to thank you for making Miss KellY a very happy person through your dedication and hard work. Your efforts and generosity are highly appreciated by the entire family.

- It is my pleasure. There is no need to thank me.

KELLY - It is so nice to see these two pretty women standing next to each other, right EdwarD?

EDWARD - Good night grandma, it's time for you leave. (He briefly kissed her goodbye.)

***

Once in the cab alone with Miss KellY, she broke down in tears.

- How could you do this to me, Miss KellY?

KELLY - I did the best fucking thing for you so far. Now you know who EdwarD really is. You don't have to believe me when I tell you to stay away from him, but you must trust your own fucking eyes.

- I want to leave.

KELLY - I know you do. In three days, you can go wherever you want. Until then, please stay with me.

- Fine.

***

That night she could not sleep, so she spent time writing on Facebook.

POST "RANDOM THOUGHTS" 21: *I am hurt right now, a lot. I love him so much and he does not love me. He loves her. I just wish to be strong enough to give up. Why can I not give up? Why do I have to love someone who does not love me? Why? I embarrassed myself in front of him many times. He thinks I am weird and he wants to stay away from me. Why did love make me crazy? How do I stop loving him? How can I forget all the good things he had done for me? How do I forget the nights when he kissed me and hugged me for hours? How do I forget his compliments and encouraging words? How do I stop blaming myself for not being able to make him love me? There is still that crazy hope that somehow he will come to see me, just that much I am asking for. At this point, I do not care how bad he talks to me, as long as he tells me something.*

He is so good-looking, smart, successful, interesting, fun, and charming. He is everything that I am not. I wish I never saw him in my life. I know I am not good enough for him, but there is still a chance that if I change, that he might want to do something with me. I have to change. I have to become beautiful and make some money, so he can look at me. Oh, my God, I wish you can know how much I love him.

***

Early that morning, EdwarD came by. She was sitting in the kitchen, staring in her tea, when he walked in.

EDWARD - Are you mad at me? (He sat across from her.)

- I am mad at myself for falling on your charm.

EDWARD - From the beginning, I kept telling you to stay away from me, but you never listened. You're the one who was after me, not the other way around.

- Thank you for making it clear that you never wanted me.

EDWARD - I wanted and I want you all the time. I just tried to avoid hurting you. I care a lot about you.

- You can never hurt me as much as I can hurt myself. How long have you been dating her?

EDWARD - I dated her for the last few years, but officially, we started being a couple a few weeks before I met you.

- Is that why you did not want to be with me?

EDWARD - I tried to be faithful to MelanY.

- How did you meet her?

EDWARD - When she started working for my mother, we bonded over the fact that we both finished law school in Yale.

- *Wow, she is educated, gorgeous and very nice, too.*

EDWARD - My mother is thrilled to have her in the family.

- *Why shouldn't she be? She is of mixed race right?*

EDWARD - She is DaN's sister's daughter. Her father is born to a black man and a white woman. Why are you asking?

- *Because we look nothing alike. I wonder which one of us is your type.*

EDWARD - Every good-looking woman is my type.

- *How original.* (She looked at him with her look filled with hope.) *What now, EdwarD? What is the next step?*

EDWARD - I can disappear from your life or we can continue our kind of love.

- *What about her?*

EDWARD - She has nothing to do with us.

- *Of course she doesn't. Let me think about all this.*

He kissed her on the lips and left.

***

The following day, she asked Miss KellY for the address of KimberlY's firm. Without question, Miss KellY gave it to her. Deep disappointment in the entire world and anger toward herself, EdwarD and Miss KellY did not allow her to see how closed Miss KellY became.

She arrived Downtown before lunch time. The company was much bigger than she expected it to be. At the front desk, she asked to speak to MelanY and a few minutes later, the two of them were alone in MelanY's spacious office.

MELANY - What can I do for you? Is Miss KellY doing well?

- She is fine. First, I want to thank you for being so nice to me. I am here to ask you something stupid.

MELANY - There is no a stupid question.

- You look amazing in your red suit. You are stylish. I love the way you talk, too. You are educated and successful. I admire you. I wish so bad to be you.

MELANY - Thank you, but I'm afraid that I don't see where you're going with this.

- I am here to ask you to leave EdwarD. (She took a deep breath.) *You can have any man on this planet. Please break up with EdwarD, so I can have my chance with him.*

(MelanY stayed calm and focused.)

MELANY - Did you ever have anything to do with EdwarD?

- No, he never even looked at me.

MELANY - I believe you.

(MelanY stood up and her voice became much louder.)

MELANY - If you ever even dream about my future husband, immigration problems and your most-likely disgusting hands will become a fairytale compared to your future hell created by me.

- Big mistake, MelanY! Big! You should have never threatened a woman who loves your man. Your cruelty inspires me.

MELANY - Be careful.

- I will, and you, too.

***

From the office, she took a cab to EdwarD's place. She waited in the lobby for him. While waiting, she played on her phone and she realized that she had a recording option. When EdwarD came, both of them went up to his penthouse and without any explanation, she started taking his clothes off.

EDWARD - So we are good?

- You should always feel great and soon I will feel the same way.

EDWARD - Let me help you feel amazing. (He put his hand under her skirt and smiled when he realized that she walked around all day long without underwear.)

- Why don't you go and get some ice so we can cool each other off?

EDWARD - I'll be right back.

He walked to the fridge and filled a huge bowl with ice. By the time he came back, she pressed the "record" button on her phone and left it on the piano keys.

- EdwarD, make love to me on the couch.

EDWARD - We'll do it on the couch, bed, counter, stairs and wherever else you want.

- You can handle that much?

EDWARD - I missed you so much that it will take me a long time before I get enough of you.

- We are connected in some weird way. All your life you will want me.

EDWARD - Show me what I will want.

She was trying to be as loud as she could. They talked dirty to each other and she made sure that he got various kinds of pleasure on the couch.

Soon he grabbed her to go upstairs with him and continue the game.

- Before we go, tell me how much you want me.

EDWARD - I wanted you so badly, ever since the day I saw you messing up your hair. Your nervousness around me was so sexy. Your warm cheeks make me shiver. I want you all the time. Many times, I even dream about you. Let me show you what you do to me in my dreams.

He extended his hand to her.

- Sexy, go upstairs, fill up the Jacuzzi and I will bring us some drinks.

EDWARD - Don't make me wait longer than two minutes.

As soon as he went upstairs, she put on her skirt and her blouse, threw her phone in her purse, and left.

***

When she arrived back to her house, she saw Miss KellY writing some letters on the kitchen table.

- *Are you hungry?*

KELLY - No, I have a present for you. It's in your room. But you can't open it until tomorrow.

- *Why?*

KELLY - I want to give you something that can protect you when I'm not around anymore.

- *Maybe I will stay with you.*

KELLY - You will not be able to stay here anymore.

- *Maybe the thing between EdwarD and I will work.*

KELLY - It never will. Help me to get ready for sleep.

***

In the morning, Miss KellY asked her to go downstairs and help EdwarD bring some boxes upstairs. She wondered why a doorman or super would not help him, but she wanted to see him.

As soon as she arrived in the lobby, she realized that she left her cellphone in her room. She gave the receptionist an envelope with a CD to be mailed to MelanY.

While she was waiting for the elevator, she heard a gunshot coming from upstairs. Suddenly, some people in the lobby started panicking and running out of the building, while the super took the emergency staircase up to investigate. She ran after them to check on Miss KellY.

When she arrived to Miss KellY's room, she found her sitting in a wheelchair; her head tilted back, her eyes open and her jaw was ruptured. The gun was next to her on the floor.

She fell to her knees and screamed as loud as she could. She crawled to her wheelchair and started to hug her bloody head and kiss her eyes.

EdwarD and the super came through the room a few minutes later. The super left the room to call the lobby and explain to them where the gun shot came from. EdwarD held a catatonic stare as he studied the situation. He walked slowly towards Miss KellY's body and her.

EDWARD - You have to leave immediately!

- I can't leave her! She might come back!

EDWARD - The police are on their way. They will ask you too many questions and try to take your information. Here, take the keys and go to my place. (He put the keys in her hand.)

She kissed Miss KellY's legs and left the room. Before she exited the apartment, she went back to kiss Miss KellY for the last time.

She found EdwarD sitting on the floor, while holding his grandma's body in his arms. He was kissing her forehead nonstop and sobbing hysterically. She turned around and left the building before police arrived.

CHAPTER 24

PAST 11

She was not allowed to attend Miss KellY's funeral. KimerlY blamed her for never suspecting what her mother was planning to do. When KimberlY called the doctors to check if her mother was taking any kind of medications, she found that Miss KellY was diagnosed with dementia that would possibly lead to Alzheimer's disease. The doctor's visits were not about Miss KellY's Botox, but about her concern for her sudden forgetting.

EdwarD brought all of her belongings to his apartment including Miss KellY's present for her. She opened the box wrapped in a silver paper in front of him. The present was a gun and two boxes of bullets. There was a note, too.

"This gun was the first one in my gun collection. You'll need it in this sick world. By the way, you'd be crazy if you would ever dare to think that I would live without my brain. Fuck Alzheimer's disease, I would never allow myself to become a vegetable."

EDWARD - She loved you very much.

- *How was the funeral?*

EDWARD - MelanY and my father were with my mother the whole time. I'm still in shock.

- *How did she end up in a wheelchair?*

EDWARD - When she was in her fifties, her car was hit by a cab. She wasn't wearing a seat belt and that allowed her spine to become permanently damaged.

- For the last few months, when she suffered the most, I ignored her.

EDWARD - We all did.

- I am so selfish.

EDWARD - She wanted you to fix your life. She always knew how to deal with her problems. You did for her what she needed from you.

- You are just being nice to me. I became too comfortable and I forgot that I worked for her.

EDWARD - If she had a problem with that, she would have told you. BarbiE, you watched her on a daily basis and you never lost respect for her. That is what she needed the most, to feel as someone important and not as poor old lady in a wheelchair. You asked her for help and advice which made her feel useful. You can't even imagine how much you bettered her life.

- Thank you, EdwarD. How about you? How do you feel?

EDWARD - Don't worry about me. I have plenty of people to talk if I want to.

***

The following day, he placed her in a hotel for a few days until she could find an apartment.

As soon as she arrived to her hotel room, she called MelanY's office. The secretary connected her shortly.

MELANY - MelanY speaking.

- Did you listen to your new CD? Sorry for lack of visuals, but I think listening to our conversation will do it justice.

MELANY - You fucking whore! You will never get my husband! I told KimberlY about your "fuck time" with her son and not only is she accusing you of neglecting her mother, but also for trying to end her son's life, too.

- While you were talking to his "mommy", I was having fun with your hubby.

MELANY - My civil wedding is tomorrow. You're invited. The police will be waiting for you.

- You could not wait for his grandma's body to cool off?

MELANY - She would not want us to change our plans and don't forget that she adored me. My wedding party will be in a few months, make sure not to miss it. (She hung up the phone.)

***

     She was in a hotel room, packing her clothes into a suitcase. She was wrapped in a cozy white bathrobe and was wearing plastic gloves. Her hair was still wet after the shower. While she was looking for the hair brush, the room was being unlocked by the card key from outside.

     EdwarD walked in wearing his gym clothes. He was wearing black sweatpants, a grey sweatshirt and dark blue sneakers. His hair was messy, sexy messy.

EDWARD - (He was furious.) Why did you give that CD to my wife?! You are crazy! You have to leave me alone, woman! I am a taken man! Step away from my wife! She has nothing to do with your and my past mistakes!

204

- Mistakes!? What the heck was a mistake?!

EDWARD - Everything! We should have never got involved. Our relationship was damaging for the both of us.

- What kind of damage did you get? What did I do to you? I loved you like God, pleased you in every imaginable way and took every kind of crap that came from you!

EDWARD - I almost lost my family's respect and my own. I should have never allowed myself to fall on your level!

- My level?! What kind of level are you talking about?!

EDWARD - You don't know anything about moral values or social structure, so I understand why you don't see the situation the same way I do.

- And she does? She is the woman who is on your level?

EDWARD - Sure she is!

- Well I might agree that both of you are on the same level, but I know for a fact that I am ten levels higher on every moral or social ladder than the both of you combined!

EDWARD - Okay, if that makes you happy, believe that yourself. I have to go.

He was about to leave the room, when she pulled out the gun from her purse and pointed it at him. The anger shaped her loud voice into a flow of crying words.

- Oh no, you will leave when I tell you what I have to say!

EDWARD - Calm down, BarbiE. Relax.

- Shut up, EdwarD! Your lovely wife, MelanY, was born and raised on Madison Avenue. The biggest problem that she ever faced was not seeing her busy mom and dad whenever she felt like it. Unfortunately, she had to be surrounded with fun nannies, housekeepers who cleaned all her mess, chefs who fed her with the best quality food, personal shoppers and the best teachers and tutors in New York State! Her worst nightmare was to be seen twice in the same designer clothes! Every good-looking and successful bachelor was available for her. She never felt rejection in any way. So, where the heck is the proof that she knows what is honorable!? You think she did not sleep with anybody!? She is not a virgin, so do not make her look like Virgin Mary!

EDWARD - Put the gun down, please. Come and give me a hug.

- Save the hugs for someone from "your level". EdwarD, I do not talk about my moral values, I live them!

EDWARD - Yes, you do.

- Do not change your opinion just because a gun is in your face. I hate women like MelanY. Those women do not have a heart. They are raised to be selfish and proud of it. Women like me raised themselves to fill their big hearts with goodness. I worked hard since I could remember. The labor by my hands was not enough and I had to give up my body forcefully and willingly for the benefit of people that I love. That is called sacrifice! Even though, I will never admit, but when you give up your body, God takes the soul! I have had sex since my childhood with more than hundreds of men who saw me as God's garbage. I had hoped that you would be the first person ever who would see me as a human being. But, you were just one

more added to my many mistakes! I opened my heart to you which was always reserved only for God. You spit on it and caused me to feel a new unknown pain! It hurts like hell being in love and not having a chance to feel for one minute how it feels to be loved in return. I begged you to give me a chance to show you what I am able to do for you and you laughed at me! Why EdwarD?! Do you think that I do not feel anything!?

EDWARD - BarbiE, I just cannot understand you or see what you see. I wish I could. (He sat on the bed, powerless.)

- Let me show a piece of my life.

She put the gun in her mouth and quickly took off both of her gloves and then pointed the gun back at him. She stretched her left hand in front of his face, forcefully.

EDWARD – Oh, my God. (He whispered)

Some fingers still had some parts of the nails, while most of them were red or pink. Some finger tips did not even have a normal shape. It was more than disgusting, especially the black tissue and loose skin at some spots.

- Yes, this is just the visible part of my life. My kidneys most likely do not have a normal shape either! Every part of my reproductive system was touched and not under anesthesia. The embryo from my uterus was pulled out by knitting needles. There is no inch of my body that was not covered by bruises. I felt sperm, urine, feces, blood, spit, alcohol, food, alkaline, wax, oils, water and tears on my skin, and most of all, I felt pain produced by my heart. Now you get to see my fingers, burned by alkaline. This visible part is nothing compared to the invisible.

(He froze.)

- To me, moral is when I wake up and feel bad for myself, because I have to live with myself another day. I still do it because I know I am able to be useful to other people. I work hard for my money and I give it with a blessing to my family and other families that I never met, so they are not forced to taste fragments of my life. Whenever I encounter someone who needs my help, I help as much as I can. Even though I can afford to eat whatever I want, I do not. I feel guilty eating when I know that there are so many people who are not even able to imagine that food can have a good taste.

(It was quiet for a moment.)

EDWARD - I need time to process all this. Please, put the gun away and let me leave.

They looked at each other in the eyes, black to green, for a few seconds, and she put the gun back in her purse. He got off the bed and quickly walked out.

She felt lighter for some reason. She placed her distorted hands back in the gloves. Then she dialed the reception desk and told them that she would be checking out tomorrow morning and that she needed a cab.

***

The morning came. She was still sleeping when she felt someone hugging her from behind. She opened her eyes and saw EdwarD holding her. He was wearing his black suit.

- Why are you here?

EDWARD - The receptionist called me to inform me about your departure. What are you planning to do, BarbiE?

- I will go upstate. I rented a trailer at a camping site and I will make my future plans over there.

EDWARD - It sounds like a brilliant plan for such a dazzling girl. You should have never given the CD to my wife. Thank God she is willing to give me another chance.

- Do you want me to congratulate to you? Where are my second chances in this life?

EDWARD - You're about to get one.

He got off the bed and walked toward the desk in the corner and picked up a large yellow envelope. He placed it on the bed next to her.

EDWARD - In this envelope, you have a debit card for one of my accounts containing half a million dollars. There is also a copy of my social security card. You will find the instructions on how to log into online banking so you can manage the money without going to the bank. I can't give you a green card, but I can give you my identity. The blue envelope contains more information about me such as the birth date, tax returns, my work information and some more details. Use this envelope's content for whatever you need it for.

- Why are you doing this?

EDWARD - My grandma always thought that there is a big potential inside you and I am unlocking it by giving you a new identity. I also arranged the cure for your visible pains.

- Money is good, but it cannot fix the hell.

EDWARD - No, it can't, but it can fix your hands in a New York Presbyterian Hospital where you are going today.

- This morning started very weird. I am not fully following you.

EDWARD - Tomorrow morning will be even weirder. (He removed the cover off her bed.)

EDWARD - You have an hour to shower and a cab will take you to the hospital. Over there, DaN will meet you and he will be next to you through the entire surgery. It took him one night to pull his connections and arrange the plastic surgery for tomorrow. In five days, you will have another hand renewed. Today you will have to take various tests.

- Are you saying it is possible for me to have normal hands?

EDWARD - They will never feel as before, but they will look the same, if not even better.

- How much is this going to cost?

EDWARD - Financially, nothing for you. I covered all the costs. But you owe me a favor.

- What can I do for you?

EDWARD - You'll take care of my BarbiE girl and make sure that she achieves her goals.

She hugged him and felt his heart beating the same rhythm as hers; too fast. He touched her on the cheek and left the room.

Her entire body became consumed with excitement. She quickly wrote an email to her family saying that she will not be able to contact them for a few days. She placed the yellow envelope inside her purse, and then jumped into the shower to get ready for the surgery. It is amazing how much happiness a surgery can allow.

This was the worst thing that EdwarD ever did for her. If he stood back this time, she would be freed forever and her life would not end in tragedy. Sometimes the kindness is the worst punishment. This act confused her even more and all of her short life, she will feel that she owes him a lot, and that she is supposed to love him unconditionally forever.

Dr. DaN waited for her at the entrance of the hospital. She was placed immediately in her room where the medical team was waiting for her. She was treated like royalty.

She was even assigned a private nurse named "MoniC" to take care of her the entire stay. She wondered how much money she was being paid by EdwarD to basically live in the hospital for a week.

MoniC was in her late twenties, very knowledgeable in her field, and extremely charming. She was a dark-skinned girl with a long black hair, chocolate brown eyes and cherry lips. Her waist was tiny with a complimenting huge bottom. It was very hard keeping your eyes away from this girl. She wondered if EdwarD or DaN slept with her yet.

After a successful first surgery, she was laying in the bed waiting with excitement to take off the bandages from her right hand, when MoniC walked inside the room carrying a cheesecake.

MONIC - Miss B., here is some real food for us. (She pulled the bed table over to her and placed the large piece of cake on it with two forks on the side.)

- I am right-handed.

MONIC - Today you need your left hand, so learn to use it.

- If you say so. (Both of them laughed while she tried to eat with her left hand.) You are an amazing nurse.

MONIC - I worked hard to achieve that status and now I'm working even harder to maintain it.

- I was watching the men when you were around and I realized that all of them cannot stop looking at you.

MONIC - Too bad for them because I don't care.

- How does it feel being successful on every level?

MONIC - I feel happy in general, therefore, everything represents some kind of success to me.

- How do you know EdwarD?

MONIC - We used to go out for a while.

- What happened? Why did it not work?

MONIC - EdwarD was fun, but I knew that I would never have a future with him because he is way too selfish. My main concern is taking care of people at work, but at home, I love being taken care of; once in a while at least.

- You broke up with him?

MONIC - We ended it in a friendly way.

- How did you meet him?

MONIC - Dr. DaN always requires having me assist him during his procedures, so when Miss KimberlY had heart surgery, EdwarD didn't leave her alone, not even for a minute. That is how we met and started our short relationship.

- I did not know that KimberlY had any health issues.

MONIC - She is really crazy and that is her main issue. (She giggled.)

- I have to agree. You know I am in love with EdwarD?

MONIC - You're a really direct woman and you don't mind jumping from subject to subject. I like that. By the way, I know you mean something to him; otherwise, he would not organize all this mess.

- You really think that he loves me? (Her eyes became shiny.)

MONIC - Knowing EdwarD very well, I know he doesn't love anyone beside himself and his mother.

- Why is it that way?

MONIC - Many rich boys are obsessed with their mommies all their lives. I wonder how MelanY is dealing with that.

- *You know her?*

MONIC - Yes, I do. We hang out in the same circles. My boyfriend works in their law firm.

- *Your boyfriend works with KimberlY, EdwarD and MelanY?*

MONIC - Yes and imagine how EdwarD feels working with those two women.

- *Do you think she is a good person and that she will make a good wife?*

MONIC - No one makes a good wife or a husband. (She giggled.) MelanY is stubborn and she'll be able to manage EdwarD very well. She is the only one who never fell on his charm. He is running after her like a puppy.

- *Great. I feel so much better.* (She took a deep breath.)

MONIC - Don't say that in a sarcastic voice. Obviously, you have some kind of an influence on him. Look what he is doing for you behind KimberlY's and MelanY's back.

- *I love him more than I love myself.*

MONIC - I love no one more than myself.

She left the hospital without gloves. Her hands felt weird but they looked so real. She could not stop looking at them.

That morning, EdwarD came to see her and he kissed each finger on her hands. He and DaN wished her luck in her life. Even though DaN was following her progress, he didn't speak a lot to her. He acted more like EdwarD's new uncle rather than someone who cared about her. MoniC gave her a large cheesecake as a goodbye present.

She promised EdwarD that she would become someone and come back to look for him. He did not comment. She was excited to start a new chapter in her life.

***

Once she arrived upstate, she decided to put into practice all of the knowledge gained from Miss KellY. Two weeks of depression actually made her stronger. She was planning to make some big money. After doing some online research, she learned that all quick money comes from sex.

She was taking a walk around the neighborhood when she found a pink and purple house in the middle of the woods. It was gorgeous. The local real estate office helped her locate the owner, who moved to Florida years ago. She presented herself as EdwarD's personal assistant and she purchased the house for him.

Weeks later, she started her new business. She knew very well that gay prostitution is not common and it is kept more secretive than any other kind of sex. She built the website and quickly found potential customers.

Her male prostitutes, the dolls, were very easy to find online. She took the bus to NYC and interviewed all the Dolls there.

On the night of the opening, all the customers were supposed to come wearing masks, so they could protect their identities. The girls at the bar were the cover, in case the police come in. It would be easier for all the customers to be accused of having sex with female prostitutes than with male ones.

After the successful opening night, many men bought a membership in her club and they visited on a weekly basis. Money was flowing into EdwarD's account. She paid him back all of the money taken for the purchase of the house. At one point, EdwarD withdrew his half a million, so all the money in the account was hers.

One Sunday, she decided to go to church to thank God for her financial blessings. The church was empty besides one elderly woman who cried in front of the altar. She approached her and found out that her name was MarrY. MarrY's family died in a car accident two years before and now she was about to lose the house that she owned because she could not pay the mortgage any longer. Without thinking, she drove MarrY to the bank and she made the entire payment on the house. MarrY loved her as her own child since that day.

***

Snow blizzards are so beautiful under the moon's light. Snowflakes are running in a circle and it looks like they want to move and stay still at the same time. They are lovely and playful. You are happy to see them, because you picture snowmen, sledding, snow fights, snow angels...Now stop and think this way: transportation delays, electricity outages, falls, school cancellations, taking off from work...Don't ever think that something beautiful can't hurt you.

The Doll House, a four year old place, is located in Oneonta, New York. It is not an easy place to find, but if you get there once, you will be able to find it a second time without a struggle. The outside of the house is pink with hints of purple around the windows.

She knew that the politician with the Phantom of the Opera mask would come that night. She was sitting in her car watching on her laptop what the cameras inside her studio were capturing.

Four years ago, when she just opened her business, she was surprised to find out how many men that she knew from TV became her customers. She used to meet them over dinner and explain to them about membership in her club. The Doll House became famous very fast.

The biggest shock was when a respectful politician made her a phone call. He requested to see her in person in her club, instead of a public place, before he gave her any kind of personal information. She refused out of fear. The same day, she received an email from him saying, "I trust you. I need this adventure in order to survive my marriage. Please, keep my secret in the name of the love that you have for my son. - JohN"

Since that day, she knew she was able to hurt KimberlY and EdwarD any minute she wanted. But, JohN, the man under the Phantom of the Opera mask, opened himself to her and she felt bad for his horrible journey with KimberlY. When DaxoN fell in love and stopped caring about the work relationship, she emailed JohN about the potential danger coming from DaxoN. She just could not hurt this man or EdwarD, even if it meant losing her own freedom.

CHAPTER 25

She was about to cover her mouth with the duct tape and end her miserable life. She was excited knowing that she will see her father, DevY, and Miss KellY in hell.

I just couldn't let her go without fulfilling her purpose in this world. And I came out...

"STOP!"

She dropped the tape on the cement.

I was suddenly able to see her entire future and I immediately regretted not letting her die that day.

But, now, it was too late, for both of us...

TABLE OF CONTENTS

TABLE OF CONTENTS, continued

BIOGRAPHY

Bojana Tokic was born in April , 1987 in Bosnia and Herzegovina. At the age of 19, she moved to the United States. Her residence is in Yonkers, NY.

She is a first time author with two more fictional books to come: "ImmigranT+OrgonE" and "OrgonE-ImmigranT".

Thank you for visiting my imaginary world...

Love,

Bojana

August, 2013